Jairus's
Daughter

Jairus's Daughter

A Midrash

Patti Rutka

JAIRUS'S DAUGHTER
A Midrash

Resource Publications
An Imprint of Wipf and Stock Publishers
199 W. 8th Ave., Suite 3
Eugene, OR 97401

www.wipfandstock.com

ISBN 13: INSERT ISBN

Manufactured in the U.S.A.

For Tommy

This book has bones

[N]o notice at all is taken of the inner disposition of the person healed....
[The miracle stories] lack, as it were, a conclusion.

Rudolph Bultmann

Acknowledgements

MANY PEOPLE HELPED THIS book come into being. I am deeply grateful to my editor, Ulrike Guthrie, for alternately prodding and massaging my muse, sometimes through the use of painting metaphors. Thank you to Dr. Ron Baard for supporting the dream, to Dr. David Trobisch for hanging on just long enough to see the manuscript breathe on its own, and to Dr. Ann Johnston for giving body to the book's spirit in the form of meetings and guidance during a busy time. I am grateful to my initial readers, the Rev. Dr. Gordon and Mrs. Marietta Andersen, who were so encouraging. Also, I am grateful to my sister, professor and poet Jean Greenwood, who has been editing my work since I was eight years old when we played "school" next to the train tracks in England. I appreciate that you didn't use red ink this time. I am grateful to Mona Jerome of Ever After Mustang Rescue, whose generous heart and seemingly tireless body care for so many horses in need. Thanks to Kris Firth for her precision, and to Christian Amondson and all the professionals at Wipf and Stock who have been so helpful in the production of what was really the first novel.

1

Capernaum, Israel, evening of the 8th of Av, C.E. 34

INSIDE, BLOOD LEAKED INTO the wool padding underneath Aviel as she lay, slack-bodied, on her pallet in the darkened house. What should have been an ordinary, cyclical exodus from her body was now life-threatening. Four days ago she had crawled to the bed in the heat of the day. Now, her once-lustrous brown curls had gone dull and her mother patted a cool cloth on her sweating forehead.

Outside, on a light, breezy day in the upper Galil of Palestine, more than thirty years after the reign of Herod the Brutal, Yohanon the carpenter sat outside his stone house carving minute detail into a scribe's table. Wind tousled his white hair as a shroud of haze fingered its way across the nearby lakeshore, covering the village of Capernaum. Cedars pointed skyward and ancient gnarled-trunk olive orchards rustled in parched pastures; their slight movement was a generous sign of life in a spring that had dried from days of still air and no moisture. Only the village's well miraculously continued to flow, even as the surrounding wadis had caked to orange-brown rock beds.

Yohanon cut into the fragrant, soft cedar to round out the table's edges, feeling the slivers fall around him. He added an embellishment at each upper corner, scrolling in olive leaves, leaving a touch of the delicate in what was to be a sturdy work tool. Considering his wrists and hands as he worked, he saw veins meandering, small blue rivers in the powdered land of his aged skin. He thought of the table's youthful future owner. Unlike his, her hands were petite, so the table was to be slightly reduced from the typical size used by male scribes; the inkwell and stylus receptacles had to be diminutive as well. Tables that fit more comfortably under the slender hands of female scribes had become his expertise, and while he couldn't sell as many of them as the regular-sized ones, he had established a reputation, and his tables had become sought after by young women trained for beautiful writing. His heart went into the making of this particular

1

table, since its future owner was his neighbor. If she recovered.

As he worked his sturdy and calloused hands into the wood, his eyes and intent turned it supple, moving it around and through his fingers. Next picking up a small cloth, he dipped it into a tiny clay vessel and spread oil over the wood, buffing it methodically. Now and then he would glance up without thinking and take in the street around him, suck his teeth, and spit out sesame seeds hidden in his gums. He spent so much time out here carving and observing that his eyes were tools themselves, penetrating the skin of his fellow townspeople to see deeper into their cares and daily incessant trials. Grief lines from years of increasing loss corralled his face, running tracks through what had been a baby face for the longest time, before his beard had grown fully.

His thoughts led him to the realization that there was respite in age, relief from the years of stupidity and the poor judgment of youthful excess. Turning from himself, concern for his young neighbor flooded him, and he wished that miracles could fall like dew this day, though he had witnessed none himself in all his life.

"Hepsabah! Some water. Please."

His wife moved in the shadows of their house and came out silently with a clay jar holding a conservative portion of water for him.

"*Baruch atah Adonai, Eloheinu melech ha olam . . .*" he began to thank God rapidly and automatically under his breath for the water they had, then caught himself and wondered why there was no specific prayer for water. Immediately he switched to the general blessing for food and drink besides wine, finishing, "*she-ha-kol nihyeh bi-d'varo*," so as to not waste an opportunity for gratitude. Indeed, he was grateful that he and his remaining loved ones were healthy, and if the denarius didn't buy what it used to, at least he was doing all right through selling his work in order to provide for his wife and their grandson. He had their gratitude, and that was all his heart needed to feel useful at his age. It was good to have settled in as a husband and father years ago, and when the children had both moved into death, then it was good to be a grandfather to their child.

Health was the greatest currency. Now, it fled the young woman down the street. The table was to be hers, God willing. While the community was small and everyone generally knew everyone else's business, there was a mystery about what ailed the small-boned, auburn-haired Aviel.

At first notice her beauty startled. She was a high-tempered darling with engraved, unending eyes, betraying that she could touch a world deeper than most. Yohanon could not have explained the power of her eyes, given the lack of grief in her life that was the usual reason for the fissures in the bedrock of a person's soul. She had shown this cavernous quality of her eyes even as a child, when she would come to sit against Yohanon's house and watch him work. They would sit silently side by side, she drawing in the dirt with a stick, he working his tools. Every once in a while she would giggle and glance up at him, and he would look into her.

"Always writing. What do you write?"

Because of his terseness, and his shock of white hair, at first when Aviel was small she had been afraid of him. She would come up close and look at all his scars—the slanted thin white line above his eyebrow, the one shaped like the lake on his forearm. His raspy questions made her pause, wide-eyed, and then she would just smile, touch one of the scars with her finger, go back to rubbing out the dust, and start writing again.

For a number of years as she grew up it was murmured that, despite her looks, she was too much like a boy, was too spirited, and that she would need to curb her tendencies to climb trees and run through the wadis with the boys, her skirts tied up around her thighs so she could throw her legs about more freely. But when she neared what should have been the time of coming into womanhood, Yohanon had observed that she did not start to separate herself off from the boys; she shunned the company of girls her age who would gather in groups to giggle and braid their hair and talk about others in undertones. She still came to stop by him as he worked, whatever the latest project on his knees. He would smile, not scold like the other adults who told her to behave more seemingly.

In bed late at night, Hepsabah, Yohanon's wife, would whisper to Yohanon the local gossip, saying that she didn't think the girl had started her cycle yet, and might not for a while because she was so physical – or maybe it was that she was so underweight. The older women knew that for some reason a girl had to have a certain amount of flesh on her to go through the regular monthly cycles; those who were too skinny never bled, nor did those, on occasion, who were more active. In any case, Aviel would still touch the boys or her father lightly on the shoulders or chest in talking with them. When her hands were not in the dirt they flew everywhere, drawing pictures in the air, as she talked and folded people into her circle, mixing and stirring her imaginative stew of human relationships.

People in the town assumed that she had not yet started as a woman, because she would have to stop touching men when that happened. Once a girl did begin her monthly cycle, she was also forbidden from going into the men's areas in the places of worship, since it could never be known for certain when a woman was in her time of ritual uncleanness. From pre-adolescence a young woman's circle became restricted to other women, but Aviel still appeared to not be bound in this way. At some point she would have to succumb to the laws.

In their private discussions Hepsabah and Yohanon had wondered if it was the sin of that freedom she took which had contributed to her current curse. No one in the town could say definitively in what way her parents must have sinned such that Aviel paid the price, because her father was a synagogue official, a Pharisee, a genuinely pious man, and a good man.

The first few days of illness Aviel had weakened, taking to her bed, pale. In the last few days, her unwellness rose to the surface as she drifted in and out of waking states. She had no delirium, but a sickness of spirit had fallen over her house, a house usually lively. Even the donkey seemed to sense something wrong and had quieted his periodic braying.

With the illness, Aviel had not come out for her normal chores, and she had stopped going to her daily scribal training. Learning this writing practice was a skill her mother and father had finally agreed was a path on which she could be encouraged, because it appeared she had a gift, and the desire to write. For all her liveliness, embedded in her writing was a profound stillness. Jairus, her father, had noticed this precious quietude that seemed to serve as a sort of breathing space from her typical rambunctiousness, even as she learned her letters as a child. Peace would cloak her as she bent over her tablet and rubbed out her mistakes with the flat end of her stylus in the wax layered on wood.

While the Pharisees valued oral tradition more than the written, Jairus recognized she had a talent that should be encouraged. So he had taken her aside one day and sat her down, given her his best stylus, pulled out a thick sheet of lower quality papyrus and the ink that scribes made from soot and gum. He added water to the mix and told her to write while her mother was out at the market. She wrote proudly, embellishing the Greek letters with the slightest of twists, detailing the thickness and thinness of each stroke precisely, writing over and over, *Theos Hypsistos*, the Most High God. Later, Jairus would teach her Aramaic and Hebrew—

even a little Latin, though as a Jew he preferred to avoid the language of their occupiers.

One day Jairus stood in the corner, behind her, watching as her small fingers deftly worked the stylus. "Perhaps . . ." her father murmured, "perhaps you could write for us, help the family," thinking of all the ways in which a scribe could be employed by Romans and Greeks in trade. "Let's not let *Eemah* know just yet," he whispered to Aviel, using the close name for her mother. "Do you like writing so very much, my little one?" She smiled secretively and nodded, then dipped the reed into the well again. "Yes, *Abba*. I prefer the ink and papyrus to the wax tablet. The papyrus talks to me," and with a crease in her young forehead she looked up at him to see if he understood.

"And what does it say?" he smiled, playing along with her as he stroked her hair.

"It says there are marks already on the page, but I must write around them so that just the right ones are revealed. Most people can't see the other hidden marks."

"Ah!" He marveled at her inventiveness.

So Jairus had approached his wife about their daughter. As her husband spoke, Rivka's eyes drifted and she raced ahead over the years to the possible paths this writing would take her daughter. After boring a hole in her husband's face with her eyes, she had gone to a cubby and pulled out a small leather purse with money. So Jairus had crossed the street to ask Yohanon to create a series of special scribal tables for Aviel as she grew, and through the years the design in the corners had reflected what Yohanon thought a young girl would like. Today, as the carpenter worked, he prayed that the table's owner would receive it in good health.

Rivka came to the door of the house and scanned for her husband, taking in the street as she raised her face to the fresher outside air. The breeze played at her prematurely graying temples. Her eyes were tired, and as she stood with them closed, praying and breathing in a single motion, she knew she would have to have some respite soon. The beauty of the day belied the desperation of her home's interior, where Aviel lay bleeding her own river.

Earlier, in the anguished pre-dawn hours filled with the prayer of birdsong, Rivka had known she would have to send out Jairus to seek help, knowing from the wisdom of women through centuries of other women dying in childbirth that her daughter had only a short while to live. It was as if Aviel was laboring to birth something from a depth within her, even though she had not even started her menstruation.

Rivka reflected that just as people had the power to hurt most the ones they loved the most, so too did blood have the power to purify, as with sacrifices, and defile, as with a woman in her menses. Blood was a duality for Jews, the core of both life and death. Blood could save, as it had when Adonai had passed over their ancestor's houses because of the blood painted on the slave doorposts of Egypt, when they were strangers in a strange land; blood could mean death through plague in that same strange land. Blood was to be respected, and feared.

Aviel wallowed in a strange land this day. Rivka didn't know what was wrong with her daughter, and the physicians didn't know either. The girl simply hadn't started her womanhood, even though her years were appropriate. Rivka and Jairus had spent exceeding amounts of money on help. In the last effort, Aviel had been examined by a renowned midwife who came all the way from Safed to the west—an experience that, when her body wall had broken, had left Aviel crying and cursing that she would never let anyone, especially a man, touch her under her skirts. Rivka had explained to Aviel what they were checking, and she had stayed in the curtained-off room during the exam, but still the girl was angry for weeks and blamed her mother for the violation. She had run through the tall grass, coming back so late one afternoon that Daniel and Nathan, two of the town's shepherds and friends of the family, had been sent out to look for her.

Now she was fifteen, and her flow appeared to have started as violently as a flash-flood down a wadi, draining her life. Spasms had wracked her light body for four days unceasingly, and she was losing so much blood into the linens and wool padding that Rivka knew she couldn't live long. It was as if the girl's life did not want to surrender up to womanhood, did not want to succumb to the cyclical weakness and down-flow of energy into the earth, even if followed by the upsurge of life and vigor. In her heart Aviel had wished instead for the steady constitution of a man, staying forever playing with the boys of her youth, and it seemed that desire was protesting through her body in bloody conflict.

When Rivka began to see her husband pacing in and out of the house like a lion in captivity, she knew it was time to send him for help – just to get him away from the iron-damp smell of blood, from the clammy skin and hollow blue-pale of their daughter's face, their beloved Aviel. She knew he would do better to take some action in his desperation, whether or not the healer Yeshua could help.

At the doorway, Rivka glanced up at Yohanon, and as his eyes turned to look a few houses down, hers followed. Jairus was just coming out of the doorway of Joseph, who made and sold water skins. Jairus nodded his head in gratitude several times and turned back towards Rivka, then broke into a trot down the dry-dust pebbled street. He stopped in front of her, and it was as if Yohanon could see red fear streaming between husband and wife.

"I need to go now, don't I?"

"Now."

"Help me with the donkey. I can't explain to the elders why I will pursue this, but God knows I've been patient . . ." He didn't need to finish what passed unspoken between them.

She was less hopeful than he for a cure; the laments of women dying as they gave birth were part of the sounds of her world. If they were ever truly going to lean on the God of their fathers, well, let them lean. She hated to have Jairus go, knowing he would most likely not be there when his daughter died, but the curtain of death descended from the hand of God, not hers. Rivka wiped her mouth and nose, her hand trembling, her ordinarily firm voice shattered. "Leave, my love. Go. Just go."

Jairus took the water skins, went around the side of the house, and slung them across Nabby, the donkey. Blinking quietly the animal stood, one hip cocked; reluctantly he roused himself for the gear-pack. Rivka disappeared again into the cave of the house and came out with a clay jar of figs and slung it across the donkey's woven blanket. Next she put a leather pouch of flat bread in a pocket of the blanket. Then she reached up for a bridle, pulling it off a hook, and held the beast's head in the crook of her arm as she slipped the bit into his mouth. Jairus went to take a last look into the darkened house, knelt and held his daughter's hand and kissed her forehead, then turned to come out to take Nabby's reins from Rivka. She held her husband tightly to her and felt his rapid breathing.

"I know Yeshua will remember you with care," she said.

"All right, let me go now."

He pressed his cheek to hers, moved the donkey out, and walked briskly alongside, not looking back.

Jairus knew how to run. Running was the only thing that had seemed to soothe him before Rivka had provided him another stable foundation, beyond the synagogue, from which to experience his own life. The sword of the wilderness had been his running ground when he was a boy, opening a vast expanse that could swallow his pain. At seven he had seen his father crucified under Herod's "cleansing"; his mother had died ten days later. The elders of the synagogue had sought him, and brought him back, where he was raised by a couple in their fifties who had survived.

So Jairus had become apprenticed to the temple at an early age, and was now a teacher. He had responsibility for the roll of scriptures that the community had paid for, and it was a particularly splendid scroll with the name of God written in gold letters. He taught classes for the older youths of Capernaum, and sometimes the younger ones, taking them to sit against the cooling rock walls on mild, sun-bleached days. There was also a small apartment next to the synagogue built for pilgrims who were coming through on their way to Jerusalem, one that included the ritual bath they used for cleansing. Jairus was proud of all that the community entrusted to him.

Yet despite all his piety, despite all his praying and begging the priests, he could do nothing for Aviel. Any difficulty in life he still soothed best by walking furiously as if to escape it physically, and Rivka knew this about him.

Once, during an argument with her, he had run out of the house, jumped onto Nabby, and kicked him into running. Jairus's legs had hung down close to the ground almost as low as his mouth was turned, and while he didn't care how ridiculous he looked to the neighbors, he did notice that though the donkey got him away from the scene faster it didn't provide the satisfaction of his long legs striding out his fury. During their arguments, Rivka and he could barely contain the volume of their voices, so the small community was aware that he was a man of passion and that she spoke freely of her convictions. In this jerk-and-tumble rhythm they moved forward in their growth as a couple, rounding their edges as they went.

Now, he walked-ran to seek the prophet they had recently brought in to speak at the synagogue, the prophet who, they had heard, was performing miracles. He was, by report, traveling only a few miles from the village, curing even the blind and the leprous. It didn't matter to Jairus how his daughter could have life—no controversy around this Yeshua concerned him. There were many zealots these days who were preoccupied with corruption at the Temple and the Jews' collaboration with

Rome's imperialism. Jairus was a devout man, and he knew at an intuitive level that the balance of his daughter's life could only be counterweighted by the power of something miraculous. He wanted it so badly he couldn't tell if he was completely falling on his face with trust before Adonai, or if he was merely begging for relief from a snake charmer.

Rivka watched her husband kicking up dust as he faded from view. She looked over at Yohanon, who worked with his back to his house in the lengthening sun. She did not lower her eyes as a woman could be expected to, but looked at him with pleading.

Yohanon put down his carving tool. He nodded towards her, and left his own head down in respect, as Rivka turned back into the house.

2

Eldorado Canyon, outside Boulder, Colorado, spring 2008

"F ALLING!"

Anna watched her fingers loosen one by one. She grimaced, but fear had no time to bloom. Peeling off the granite rock face she noticed the delicate quality of the warm air rushing past her skin. Falling was a rare and perversely delicious moment of complete letting go to space and gravity. Her body's pull swung her out on the rope as she sailed soundlessly through the air before meeting the harness, which yanked at her waist.

Dangling in the air one hundred eighty feet off the ground, she groaned and looked around. The iron warm taste of blood dripped over her upper lip onto her tongue.

"You okay?" came a faint, disembodied shout from her partner at the other end of the rope up above an overhanging portion of rock.

Anna didn't answer. Problem one: she was inverted and twisted. It wasn't good. After four minutes blood flow would begin to decrease to her head, then she would pass out. The other problem was her head gash. Off her harness hung several pieces of metal called protection, used for placement in small cracks in the rock. One of these pieces had hit her in the forehead when she fell. Sweat mingled with the blood and began to tickle her nose.

She looked up and noticed the hot blue sky gathering pillows of darkening clouds. El Dorado Canyon outside of Boulder, Colorado, was famous for its late summer afternoon thunderstorms, and it looked like today would follow the pattern. A few gloppy drops began spattering.

Anna flexed her forearms, then her hands and fingers, which were bound in protective athletic tape so she could jam her hands into cracks in the rock, gain more friction, and not tear up her skin. She contemplated the possibility that the rope was jammed in a crack above her head about twenty feet up. Because her body weight was hanging on the rope, she knew she could pull on it to right herself, but she also risked dislodging

10

the rope enough so that she would jerk down another several feet. That friction was bad: it could sever the rope. But she had to do something, and soon, because it was getting harder to raise her chest to breathe and she didn't want to be light-headed as she attempted to climb again the portion of the rock off which she had just fallen.

She reached up for the multicolored ten-and-a-half-millimeter rope made of the stuff that went into plastic bags and car bumpers and prayed she was making the right move. Her biceps flexed and she splayed her feet out on the rock beneath her. The rope held; she got a purchase with a fairly good foothold underneath her.

Lightning cracked in the distance. Anna counted under her breath, each five seconds representing a mile between the center of the storm and her. Two miles away. There was no chance now of hearing her partner above her until after the storm stopped. She would need to be able to hear her partner confirm the short command of her "up rope!" as she climbed, but if the rope jammed farther above and her partner could not hear her, then the rope would not ascend and stay taut on her harness. Her spine curved uncomfortably as she settled into the awkward stance on the small foot ledge she had found. The bulk of the storm would have to pass. As she waited under the small overhang above her, she closed her eyes to let the warm rain mingle with the blood from her head and run in stream-lets down her sweat-soaked body. When she opened her eyes a moment later, she realized there was rain-melted pigeon crap from the crack above coming down. Her stomach heaved.

"I do this because . . . why?" she muttered to herself.

But she knew the answer that was wedged into a deep inarticulate place inside her like a hidden treasure: the rock never changed. That is, almost never; on rare occasions there could be some shifting and slight rock fall, or a loose hold, but it was rare. The rock was an intimate and private place that held her trust. She climbed because she placed her faith in rock, trusted that it had been there for a very long time and would continue to be there for a longer time after she was gone. She cringed when she saw roads blasted through rock ledges on highways that had been put through mountains, but here, in the protected wilderness areas, the rock was pristine and untouched, except for the climbers who had gone before her.

Most rock felt good under her hands. Granite was best, because of the friction it provided, as well as its solidity; mica schist and basalt tended to be a little more slick, and hardened volcanic ash, such as at Smith Rock in Oregon, would tear at a climber's fingertips after a single day, leaving raw skin. Exploring a rock's surface was, she imagined, like a blind person exploring the features on a person's face. She could know the rock, and the rock was solid; it was simply there, acknowledging her silent probing. She supposed answers came to her questioning hands in their own time, more likely when she was off the rock rather than on it, and she rested in that knowledge.

The rain began to lighten and she wiped her face on her shoulder. She looked up again, worried about getting the pigeon junk in her eyes. Uncertain if the rope was jammed or not, she wavered in her decision to climb again. She had fallen only because she had ignored the flaming pain in her forearms, simply wanting to get this particular climb over; it wasn't that the climb was beyond her ability. In fact, she could have led it, so that she would have been at the top now instead of her partner. They had decided to try it despite the known weather hazard, but he owed her one on account of the pigeons.

She climbed a few feet. The rope did not rise with her, remaining slack at her waist. Nervous at this development, because another fall with slack rope this time would hurt a lot more than a fall with a rope tight on her, she yelled "Up rope!" at the top of her lungs. The rope didn't answer.

"Up rope! Up rope!" Still nothing. She would have to climb another foot, try to dislodge the jam.

She found another small ledge for her feet and stacked them side by side, then yanked on the rope for all she was worth. Blessedly, it came loose. Her partner was awake at the other end and hauled it up until it was snug again at her harness. She shook out her arms, dipped her hand into the chalk bag at the back of her waist, then realized in dismay that she had left it open during the rain storm so that the chalk had gummed up and was now useless. The rock was wet anyway, she realized, and she would just have to make do. Wending her way through the cracks, using each fissure to her balance and leverage advantage, she snaked up the rock. Her focus distilled as she blocked out all other sensory input to complete the harder section near the top.

Her forearms were on the edge again for lactic acid build-up, but now she calculated how much strength she had left and decided to make the final lunge for the top. Her fingers grabbed a nub, she worked her feet onto a good hold, then proceeded to put to shame a Barbie doll's flexibility as she pulled up and over the top of the climb like she was getting out of a swimming pool.

Jonathan, looking like a bedraggled rat, his legs braced against the ground, widened his eyes at the blood, then smiled at her when he realized her flying accusations were sign enough she was okay.

"How'd you like that finish?" he said.

"Just ducky. I had pigeon poop dripping in my face. And the rope was jammed."

"Yeah, I figured. I kept tugging and tugging after you fell and you just weren't moving for the longest time, so I figured there was a jam. Guess you undid it, huh? Good thing. I'd trade you the pigeon poop for being a lightning rod up here."

She smirked at him, then rubbed her forefinger and thumb together. "World's tiniest violin."

"Good climb, but it would have been a lot better if it had been dry," he offered.

She just shook her head. They began coiling the rope and organizing the metal gear pieces before hiking out for the last day of their vacation before the drive home to Wisconsin across the Badlands.

3

JAIRUS ALTERNATELY RAN AND walked. The dust and grasses whispered to him while his legs tensed and his toes flexed; he moved under the burning blue of the Galilean sky but did not notice it. Nabby's ears wiggled away flies, as Jairus's anxieties whirled around him. Gradually, he and the animal moved into a rapid rhythm.

He had had to leave in a hurry; Aviel was dying and his further delay would only make him responsible. Thus, it was in an unclean state that Jairus sought Yeshua. "It can't be helped," he explained to the donkey, needing to engage with something living besides the thoughts in his head. "One small drop of blood, an entire well, who is to know? I had to leave, and even now, who knows . . ."

Aviel's bleeding worried him from more than just a health perspective. Jairus knew thoroughly how he had violated the laws of purity these last few days, with his caresses of Aviel's brow, his holding her hand. He should never have touched her in the first place, should have left it up to Rivka and Devorah, their youngest, to care for her. But every inch of his skin knew his touch could be life-giving to his dearest daughter, and so, in the privacy of his own house, he had done what he believed any father, Greek, Roman, Jewish, Samaritan, would have done. *Pekun nefesh.* Saving a life. No one would know except his family. And maybe Yeshua. Jairus decided to keep it to himself, until he could speak to Yeshua himself, take him aside.

Jairus would go to the *mikvah* ritual bath to cleanse himself when he returned. Back at home, Jairus's synagogue was sizeable and did well financially, although Jairus was grateful he did not have to handle the monies. His responsibilities suited him: he led a study group for the youngest of students each day and was helping to plan the construction of a school for them. Through study God could speak to people, Jairus believed, and through prayer the people could speak to God, so he also led the daily services, kept them on time, prepared and sometimes read from the scroll, and helped the young readers be less nervous as they read. Often he would hold a calming hand on their shoulders as they pointed to the Hebrew words with the silver *yad*, the miniature pointer designed in the shape of a hand, intended to mark the place for the reader without the reader having to touch the sacred scroll. He made sure the scroll was put away properly with its ornamentation and coverings and took responsibility for a myriad of details that were so ingrained in him that he could not imagine not caring about ritual. Ritual, along with Rivka's solid support, allowed him to bring into line his sometimes chaotic internal world.

Jairus reflected on the distinguishing nature of ritual. Through ritual Jews became different from the Greeks and Romans, as they sanctified the mundane tasks of life along with the voracious appetites of sex, love, power, and wealth. The holy mysteries of life and death they acknowledged through the letting of blood in animal sacrifice at the Temple. Ritual's framework created a space in which, gradually and over time, Jairus could feel his responses to the world. He was a thoughtful, sensitive man, which others seldom guessed, and he loved his wife and daughters.

This illness of Aviel's had no structure. It fit within no framework he knew. It was as foreign to him as working on a Sabbath would have been. In ritual he could find meaning; in this impending death, nothing. Because he allowed small but expanding room for mystery beyond the meaning provided by ritual, he sought Yeshua.

When Yeshua had come to speak at Jairus's synagogue, it was as if, when he spoke, even when he read from the scripture, a new framework took shape, ether-like, but nonetheless real. Jairus wasn't sure he could grasp the new inflection Yeshua placed upon the scripture, the way he seemed to make oral side-notes in the margins to the ancient teachings. His teachings were sand and water at the same time; they were baffling yet made the brokenness of life take on a wholeness that even the simplest of people could understand.

And the reaction Yeshua had caused in the synagogue! "You should have seen it, Nabby. They fell over themselves. A bunch of white-haired old men more concerned about what Yeshua picked out of his fingernails than about the heart of what he said." The Pharisees had mumbled amongst themselves, not while he read, of course, but after, in small conspiratorial gatherings intended to be invisible. The women, who gathered in colorful, flowing groups seemingly propelled by their own chitterings, accepted Yeshua's teachings twofold: for the draw, the power, which seemed to emanate from him, and for the comfort of the words themselves, which reminded them of the words they told their frightened children on the darkest of deep star nights. Jairus suspected that it was in fact that very power of Yeshua's against which the men reacted, the very learned ones to whom Yeshua seemed to direct so much of his intention.

But it didn't seem right that the message the young rabbi brought them should cause so much consternation. Prophets had never been exactly welcome in his people's history; they had always brought lessons as if to ill-behaved children, and who wanted to hear that? Yet there were the stories of healings, in addition to the teachings, that had been making it around the region. When the Bedouin sheepherders came through, passing by local wells, they would tell of the miraculous dealings this man Yeshua trailed behind him.

"If he can restore the withered hand of a man, and a paralytic, and a leper, what else can he do for Israel? Free us of Rome?" some had begun to ask when he came to teach.

Jairus had hesitated to ask Yeshua personally when he had had the chance that Sabbath in Capernaum. And even when Yeshua had agreed to come to Jairus and Rivka's house after the service to bless the bread and wine, Jairus had remained quiet, simply listening. Aviel and her younger sister Devorah had remained so quiet, so well-behaved; Jairus was proud of their decorum. They were good girls, and yet so different. Aviel was more like a boy in the way she carried herself, while Devorah was smaller, more feminine; it would be easier to find a husband for her. Unlike Aviel, she did his and Rivka's bidding without complaint. And she was especially devoted to Aviel. It would perhaps hit her the hardest when her sister died, and he knew there was nothing she would spare for her sister.

Jairus's reflections receded, and as he and the donkey neared the north end of the lake Nabby's ears picked up a crowd of people in the distance. His heart wrenching, Jairus thought of Aviel, and his mind again drove itself in circles, looping back and back again on what could be happening with his daughter. He alternated between talking out loud to the donkey and praying silently to Adonai for help.

As Jairus came closer, he saw the crowd grow larger and more colorful. People crowded around the central speaker, whose voice belled with clarity; his hands gestured as if he would press and knead every word into them. The bright sun glinted off the lake, and a wind blew in, heaping the water in white piles out farther from the shore. The air wafted a fresh green algae lake smell. A fisherman's boat might easily be swamped and sink in these conditions. Jairus had been right about where to look for

Yeshua, and it had only taken him two and a half hours to reach the spot on the lake.

As the donkey and the man closed in on the group, the speaker looked up and paused in the story he was telling the group. He seemed to recognize the synagogue leader but continued with his teaching.

Jairus fixed his eyes on Yeshua and moved through the people; he absently handed the reins of the donkey to a young boy standing at the edge of the crowd and continued on through the rest with a singleness of intent that connected him as with a cord to Yeshua. At one point he stumbled, but still he moved forward, parting the bystanders with insistent hands.

As people moved out of the path of his pressing need, he arrived a few feet from the teacher. Yeshua paused, and looked at him. A small circle in the dust had opened before Yeshua, and into this space of hope and belief Jairus prostrated himself. Jairus knew a Jew did this only once a year, on Yom Kippur, the Day of Atonement, bowing to no one the remainder of his days, worshiping only the God of Israel, so he was not surprised to hear the crowd mutter.

"Sir, I come to you to beg your help. My little daughter lies at the point of death. I . . . Please . . . come back with me and lay your hands on her. I know your hands and your words can heal her." He looked up, his throat dry, but his eyes pools of yearning. Then he looked back down at Yeshua's feet, his heart lolloping loudly over his scrambled thoughts. Fixed on the ground, his eyes noticed the earth and filth in Yeshua's toenails, the length of his toes, brown at the knuckles with the dust of the day.

Yeshua knelt down before Jairus, his plain, roughly woven robe folding over and covering his toes. He contemplated the man, the leader of a synagogue, and took in the man's desperation. How men suffer! he thought. He reached out, placing his hand on Jairus's solid shoulder, which was clothed in the best embroidered linen of the day. Jairus felt a pull to look up, but he could only look at Yeshua's chin as the prophet spoke.

"Do not fear. Only have faith."

Then, Yeshua stood and turned to John. His lanky, beloved friend sat nearby and watched the exchange with quick young eyes. "We'll go to help this man's daughter. As we walk, I'll continue teaching, if they follow," gesturing toward the crowd with his head. "Be good enough to bring some of that fish." In the early morning hours Yeshua and his disciples

Peter, John, and James had taken the nets out and caught enough for a few days of meals.

Taller than Yeshua, John nodded and lifted his bronzed frame, then joined the sturdier Peter and slighter James, and the remaining disciples. They began to gather up fish, water skins, and leather pouches of figs and olives, slinging them over their shoulders. As a flickering unit they moved, flocking like waterfowl in flight, fanning out behind the one in the lead.

Suddenly, a man in the moving crowd shouted, "Why this man's daughter?" He was too young to have a face as sour as he did. "Why not my uncle, a leper whose flesh rots off him and stinks up the linens and salve wrapped around his face? Why not the neighbor boy, who stutters so badly the children mock him and pelt him with stones? Is this man special because he runs the synagogue?"

Peter and James began to shoulder their way through the crowd towards the man, though Yeshua kept walking.

Looming large in the bitter man's direction, Peter snarled, "Yeshua blesses whom he chooses! Would you place yourself in the position of being the one to choose, the one to decide who receives God's forgiveness of sins? Be grateful you don't have the responsibility! Who are you? Where are you from?" Peter was imposing, and he wanted the man to feel his presence.

"If his message is so very important, why doesn't he take it to Sepphoris, or Tiberius, ten times the size of miserable Capernaum!" harassed the man in a last attempt. But the crowd buzzed around his bile and he slunk off.

Yeshua simply kept moving, now with Nabby and Jairus alongside him. Who chose to be in the following group came along.

They moved quickly, death pressing them through the dry land. After a short while, Yeshua abruptly stopped and looked down.

"I feel—odd." Light played across his face. Peter came alongside him, and Yeshua looked at him and asked, "Who touched me? Who touched my garments?" He wasn't angry, just puzzled. He turned and scanned the faces of the people around him.

"You see all this crowd around you, and yet you're asking who touched you?" At times Yeshua's quirks frustrated Peter, and it was hard for him to reconcile the otherworldliness of the prophet with some very real annoyances about a person many said was simply odd.

Yeshua stood, still looking about him. A woman a few layers back in the crowd came and knelt before him, afraid to look at him directly.

"It was I, rabbi! I'm sorry! Please forgive." She wrung out her words. "I knew if I reached out to you I would be well. For twelve years my life has drained. I know I am forbidden from touching you. I know. But I thought, I said to my companion, I thought, if only I could touch even the hem of his garments, I would be healed. I knew this. In my heart. Right here." She thumped the center of her chest with her fingers. Then she flung out her arm and pointed. "I have paid out money to every physician and every wizard in this area and beyond, and I am destitute. But I knew you could heal me. I've heard the reports."

She had been miserable for years, but she'd had enough life in her to seek out the healer. Her words had taken on a growing intensity. Then the flow of her words ceased, and she reached down and pressed her hand against her dress, between her legs, and began to cry at the new dryness she felt there. People were again still, marveling at the brazenness of the woman coming to touch Yeshua while she was in such a state of ritual impurity. Would he have to go to the Temple for cleansing, or could he himself forgive her?

Yeshua reached down to her arm and pulled her square to face him. The crowd moved back a little and again hummed among itself, then was silent as the man and the woman stood looking at each other.

"How do you feel now?"

"Alive," she offered, a deep peace welling up from within her.

"Daughter, your faith has made you well. Go, peace to you, be healed of your dis-ease."

She began to recede in the crowd, laughing and raising her arms in the air in praise, looking back in Yeshua's direction, knowing she was not only healed but also forgiven and purified.

Peter frowned and shook his head again, knowing that this kind of display carried farther in the word-of-mouth circles than the deed itself. Here was another one that would continue spreading Yeshua's already sizeable following, and his fame. It wasn't as if there was anything he could do to prevent Yeshua from acting this way, and of course he wouldn't, but it seemed as if Yeshua was usually oblivious to the consequences. More irritated than amazed, the disciple turned to the fellow with whom he had been talking and asked, "Do you know this woman? Is she typically so bold?"

"I have heard she's indeed been bleeding for twelve years, nearly constantly, and that her deceased husband left her enough money to live on. But she exhausted her wealth—and the patience of all the physicians around, as well as some outlandish practitioners from away. You know, east of us. Damascus, even. What and whom she has not consulted I certainly don't know. Her family abandoned her, and I think, perhaps, she's been more nearly dying of loss of love—and someone to talk to—than loss of blood." He looked around him and continued in an undertone, "Women especially come to seek out your Yeshua. Me, I think it's a lot of charisma he has, no disrespect intended to you." He shrugged, not sure if he had spoken too honestly.

"Ah. It is so very much more than charisma." Peter smiled, and reflected on the phenomenon of the man to whom he had bound himself. He trusted that Yeshua knew what he was doing. "You watch. You wait. You'll see. Yeshua is—Yeshua is Messiah," and he turned back to make sure the woman had cleared her way through the crowd to leave. He often thought of himself as Yeshua's bodyguard, and again shook his head. Even though Yeshua might be the Savior, he was a little stupid sometimes, in a practical sense.

Jairus had both marveled and grown impatient with the woman's interruption. He was relieved when she left and the group had continued on.

Every breath of movement they made might make a difference to Aviel, and if Jairus had had a whip, he might even have used it to drive the entourage forward faster. Ever steady in the distance, the lake sparkled as they came closer to Capernaum. It was all Jairus could do to keep from breaking away from the group and running into the village, to his house.

Just then Daniel and Nathan, the two shepherds from Capernaum, came sweating and running up to the group. Jairus felt his throat constrict, and he looked warily at Nathan, whose flat expression he had never been able to fathom.

"Jairus, sir! Sir . . ." Daniel, the elder of the two, his face so plain it was beautiful, came up to the father and grasped his wrist as he went down on one knee. "Sir. Sir. Your daughter has died. There is no need for the healer. Your wife has brought in the mourners. I am—so very sorry." He barely got out his words because he had loved Aviel since they were children and they had played together, running the sheepdogs into frenzies in the pastures. He looked pleadingly at Jairus, tears in his eyes.

A raw blade cut Jairus's breath. He stood in silence, working his jaw, looking at no one.

Yeshua came over to Jairus. He didn't have to muster force or power behind his words; he was simply, impossibly, directing the scene. "As I said to you before: do not fear. Only believe. There is love, and there is fear. You love your daughter."

Jairus's face contorted and he could only nod once, his frame turned as if to straw and dust.

Yeshua again put his hand on Jairus's shoulder and waited for him to follow along, then turned to Peter and said, "Only you and James and John. Make the others wait here." Peter followed Yeshua's orders and took charge.

They were only half a mile out of the village, and, as they drew nearer, Yeshua propped up Jairus as he stumbled along. Already they could hear the lamentations of the wailers.

A circle of women who were barefoot and had their hair down moved first left, then right, wailing in antiphony around one older woman in the center. Two flute players stood off to the side, piping the dirge tunes that announced a death. Only one of the women cried in earnest, Hepsabah, Yohanon's wife, while the others were simply somber-faced, performing their duty. The weight of grief hung heavy in the air.

Yohanon sat on his stool outside his house, his tools on the ground. Tears glittered in his eyes, and his hands lay flat on his lap, as if dead themselves.

Yeshua stopped outside Jairus's house and the weepers.

"Why do you weep?" he said quietly enough so that it undercut the lamentation. "Why the tumult? This child—" and here he looked at Jairus, who was frozen outside his own door, and Rivka, who clung both to the doorway and her husband's face—"this child is not dead. She is only sleeping." He pronounced each word with emphasis. Aviel was beyond the age of being a child, and Yeshua knew it.

Rivka looked at Yeshua and blinked, her eyes swollen. Tears welled up again as the cruelty of Yeshua's words hit her. Silently she shook her head, her mouth twisting as she began crying harder. Why would he say what was not true? Her daughter was dead!

But one of the dancing women in the circle, young, and with little in her head, started laughing at Yeshua. Next the flute players joined in, and soon the whole group of supposed mourners was ridiculing Yeshua as he stood in his light linen robe and scuffed sandals, his hair obviously unwashed and unoiled. They would have laughed at any miracle worker without his reputation, of which they were unaware.

Turning from them, the healer stepped into the doorway, coming so close to Rivka that she could smell his pleasant and mild, earthy body odor. Overwhelmed by both her grief and now his magnetic presence, she briefly remembered that she should offer him the fragranced oil to daub on his forehead and a clay bowl of water to rinse off his feet. Instead, she stepped aside. He looked in, told the other women and the young girl already in the house to go out and leave them, then he turned back to Jairus. Taking Jairus's hand, he placed it in Rivka's.

"Come in with me. Peter, James, John, come in here," he called out the door to the three. John looked at his brother, and Peter cleared his throat.

They all entered the darkened house.

4

AVIEL LET GO AND slid down into floating, restful dark. Peace enveloped her. Others, many others, were nearby, also at peace, a multitude surrounding her in ceaseless shadow, gliding over and around one another. She had held on tenaciously, not wanting to release her soul from her body, but now, here—wherever here was—she knew she could float forever, blessedly free of the sweat and torque, the grinding pain slicing like shattered glass inside her body in the last hours of her life. Finally, the last sinew was cut. It was all she desired. The relief was a bliss enduring, unending, a final freedom. Eternity.

But then she felt the oddest of sensations: she was sinking up, into a transparent vessel of water, daylight at the top, her body pulling her back to the light and to the pain, as if to die again. A loud pop! and again she felt the crushing in her abdomen, along with a burning in her hand. Her hand was on fire as the light grew brighter. She twisted around towards it, then heard a resounding command in the center of her chest—a man's voice:

"Little girl, get up!"

She gasped, jolted into her body, and arched on the pallet. In the radiance of the healer's presence, and the heat of the day, she perspired. A strand of her hair stuck to her face. His fingers moved to pull the hair from her mouth; he wiped the spit from her cheek and cradled one side of her face in his warm hand. Then he touched her abdomen. Pain seared through her body cavity again but began to subside rapidly. Miraculously. She blinked, her eyes crusted with tears, and she looked hazily toward the figure holding her hand. He was so bright!

Yeshua took her hand and placed it over her heart, pressing it to her. As he let go, she struggled up toward him, not wanting him to release her, not wanting to come back to the pain of existence. But he did, and his brilliance dimmed. Before her stood a man in a plain wool robe covered with dust, smelling lightly of sweat and earth and fish. There were others around, men she did not know, different from the beings in the floating space from which she had just returned. She recognized her father and mother, her *Abba* and *Eemah*.

Rivka crushed Jairus's hand in hers, tears swelling her eyelids again. Jairus looked at Yeshua, but devoid of shock; he was simply and strangely vacuous, because his entire underpinning had shifted. It was as if his house had slid off to one side in an earthquake, and it was unclear if the house would remain standing with this new knowledge of belief and faith. He let go Rivka's hand, slid down the wall to squat on the floor, and stared at his daughter in the darkened room.

Outside, the commotion of wailing and ridicule that had greeted Yeshua before he went into the house had muted, and the crowd of family and friends convened, talking about the miracle worker Jairus had gone to seek. A sweetness of figs filled the warmth of the day, and the dust under foot was somnolent, heavy with heat. The shroud of haze from the lake had receded.

Back inside, Yeshua directed Aviel, "Go cleanse yourself at the *mikvah* when you've gained more strength, and present yourself to the priests." Then he turned also to Jairus and Rivka so that they were drawn into reminding their daughter about her obligations.

Weak, Aviel turned on her side and pushed herself up off the pallet, her lightweight woolen robe clinging to her shape from her sweat. She swallowed, and swung her feet cautiously onto the floor to test her weight on her legs. Putting her arms behind her on the bed she pushed herself up to rise, and Yeshua and John moved as one to help her, Yeshua's hand under her arm, John's hands awkwardly and a little too familiarly at her waist. Did they know she had dried blood sticking her legs together, pulling her skin? These men should not be touching her; she was unclean for them, she worried.

Rivka rushed to her to take over, supporting her daughter's weight, pushing her hair off her forehead, kissing her. "Aviel! Aviel, Aviel."

Standing alongside Rivka, John had not let go.

Yeshua spoke. "If one is forced to choose between the law and saving a life, wouldn't you agree that it is more important to save the life?" The healer smiled at Rivka and John, then turned to Jairus. "Feed her. If your girl is to become a woman, she needs to keep up her weight, and she is to do the ritual cleansing once she is restored. Remember what I told you: do not fear. Only believe. She will find her life through words more than childbearing."

Jairus looked at him blankly, and before he could expound his gratitude, Yeshua left with a blessing. Feeling conspicuous, John relinquished his hold on the young woman and followed Yeshua, his eyes trailing to Rivka and Jairus as he went out.

Rivka turned to watch them go, but could not release her daughter; she began laughing and crying at the same time. But Aviel wriggled out of her mother's arms and stumbled to the door, gripping it with her hands. As she looked fuzzily out into the clearing day and towards the men departing with Yeshua, she saw John, tall, moving gracefully.

Sensing her gaze, John stopped, turned, and met her eyes. In each other they recognized a depth. While they entered each other's souls mutually, Aviel was still in the weaker state. The intensity of his penetration spiraled up in him, moving from a spiritual depth to a hunger for human love. But Aviel was so close to her humanness, having just regained it, and at the same time so close to that world of spirit she had touched, that she did not have the strength to continue bearing his gaze. She looked down. When she looked back up, wanting more, she saw his eyes had just left hers.

He had turned back to follow Yeshua and Peter and James. She watched him go, then sank to her knees, still holding the doorway for support. Too much life flooded back into her all at once, and Rivka came over to her, frowning up into the street.

Aviel stared down at her left hand. It was tingling and burning.

He'd done it again. Peter wondered what the reaction would be this time. Would he go to the *mikvah* after touching that girl? The crowd outside the house had informed Peter of the girl's —woman's—condition. He knew he worried about too many things for Yeshua's sake, but really, there needed to be no controversy about this, about whether or not she was a full woman, in her unclean state. Yeshua had already caused enough consternation healing a man's hand on the Sabbath, and now this had happened at the house of a Pharisee! If his Lord kept doing these healings there would be trouble with the authorities. He turned to see John behind him, looking back at the house. What he saw was Yeshua's favorite exchanging looks with that girl.

John, however, trailed like a straying and distracted sheep. He glanced up at the hard blue sky, feeling the dryness of the last several weeks in his mouth. He looked again at the group of three moving away from him, then glanced again at the house. Aviel's house was quiet, impressed upon his mind. He came along tighter to the others, falling in and listening as Yeshua talked.

As the four of them walked back out of the town, a young man in a robe covering caved-in shoulders skulked near by, hovered, and when Yeshua passed nearby he spat at the healer, turned, and ran. A neighborhood boy cried out and chased the man, throwing a few stones at him, while some other villagers standing in doorways as Yeshua moved past said out loud, "Don't mind him." "We know the good works you come to do—we see! Never mind the crazies." James came a little closer as they walked and spoke in low tones into Yeshua's ear. Yeshua's mouth turned up at the corner, and he looked sideways at his brother as they padded through the dust. They needed rain.

When Yeshua spoke again, his words swam over John, seining in the disciple's loose ends, pulling his heart back to the feel of the group. John's elation rose, filling like a balloon made of papyrus sheaf and filled with hot air from a delicate light lit underneath. It floated up into the deepening Galilean dusk. Still, he couldn't forget the young woman he had just seen. Coming up close beside Peter he found comfort in his large presence. Not wanting to betray the light of interest in Aviel that flickered in him, he nonetheless felt compelled to get any information he could about her.

"Did Yeshua know Jairus from before that Sabbath we came through Capernaum?"

Peter looked sideways at him.

"I don't know—but I don't think so. Does he interest you?"

"I am still stunned by some of the things Yeshua says and does," John hedged. "I wonder about the family. I wonder how what Yeshua does affects them later. Especially the women. The young woman—what was her name?"

"Aviel, he told me."

"Yes, Aviel, that's right, I heard her mother. Aviel—what will her life be after what Yeshua has done for her? What becomes of these people whom Yeshua touches in the ways he does?"

Peter only shook his head. His concern was less with the people Yeshua healed than with how the healings had an impact on Yeshua's message and mission. As a whole, the disciples had become as accustomed to the miracles as any human being could, but still, doubt would ripple through them on occasion. Apparently John had been more affected by this one than some of the others. At least, that was what he hoped was the cause for John's interest.

They had come to a stopping place for the evening near the lake once again, and the followers that had adhered to them once they left Capernaum began to find places in small groups to lie down for the night. This time lack of rain was in their favor, so they had decided not to go all the way to Nazareth that day; they would have enough time to arrive by sundown for the next day.

The disciples placed their blankets on the dry ground and began to pull out the wine and water skins and the bread that had been patted flat by women's hands and baked on the large inverted metal ovals used for baking. Having said the blessings for wine and bread, and only sprinkling droplets of water in lieu of fully washing their hands because water was so scarce, they tore off and chewed the thin, crusty pieces, added a few olives, and washed it all down with the wine. Once the simple meal was concluded they began to chant the Hebrew thanksgiving prayers, and this easily continued for an hour. Their song carried out across the water on the dying wind as the stars began to appear in a crystalline cool sky.

Reclining on his blanket, John looked up at the evening star and laid his head on James' shoulder. He felt his brother's breathing, his chest rising and falling, and he wondered if the young woman to whom he had been so drawn was rejoicing in seeing the stars again after so nearly dying.

That night, John dreamed of blood washing up on the shore of the lake as a wind whipped the blood-water into a pink froth. Fish beached by the thousands, and scores of lepers, demoniacs, cripples, people with every kind of disease, came to gather the fish, throwing them in the air and catching them with their mouths, then eating them. Yeshua and Aviel loomed large together, coming down out of black billowing clouds, Aviel clothed only from the waist down in exotic foreign yellow silk, and her long hair. Yeshua disappeared; Aviel settled near John, stars all around her, as he lay like stone, unable to move, on the beach. Then, feeling himself between his legs, he woke throbbing in the early dawn. The sense of her in the dream stayed close with him throughout the morning as the group continued moving and talking alternately of the old prophets and the political situation on the way to Yeshua's home town.

5

Madison, Wisconsin

"**O**H FOR CHRISSAKE!" BACK in her apartment in Madison, Anna slammed shut the laptop and turned to the cat, who had just about figured out the rudiments of speech. "What good does it possibly do to be 'saved' if you're so depressed you fall over your own feet?"

Anna kicked the cat's green jingle play-ball and swept away some coffee cups and crumpled papers from her third-floor apartment desk as she continued to spout off about the e-mail from her high school girl friend Paula. Like her thoughts, Anna's personal belongings took on a whirlwind life of their own. She was a pigpen unto herself.

"Anti-depressants, maybe? Therapy? Ya think? Might help a little. Why is it so many Christians have this disconnect between what they say they believe and how they conduct their lives? It's as if once they're saved, people expect Jesus to do all the work for them. Don't they realize they're creators within their own lives? I mean, if they can accept that Newton's laws of physics work to keep their feet on the ground," and here she paused in her tirade to make sure the cat was still listening, "why can't they accept that the new laws of physics might actually work too, in terms of how their thoughts affect their lives? The observer has an affect on what is observed! The metaphor is so elemental! It's not like if you say you have the power to create a lot in your own life that there isn't room for Jesus anymore. Or like saying that you're actually God. If God had meant us to fly he'd have given us wings, right? So goes the thinking. Man. People need to get help. Like psychotherapy, for example. Understanding how quantum physics works is a tool, just like therapy and medication and surgery are tools. God gave it all to us."

If pressed here, she couldn't have given a concise set of her beliefs about God, but she continued on her private rant. "That includes the ability to think creatively and positively. Which is something you're definitely not capable of," she said to the cat. The cat, if he had been able to think, would have wondered about the contents of the offending e-mail.

Anna shoved back her chair and headed for the shower. She didn't really expect an answer from the cat, who showed large incisors in a yawn while stretching out a paw in her direction, but she had gotten so used to talking to herself out loud that she didn't worry anymore about her sanity. The cat certainly didn't seem to be a cocreator in his reality. After all, his brain was only the size of a tennis ball, so how much processing capacity could there be in there?

Anna hummed, "Good-bye Norma Jean, though I never knew you at all . . . ," turned on the hot water in the shower, and watched the bathroom mirror steam over as she undressed and hung her pungent stable clothes on the back of the door. Stepping in, she wondered first why the last song she heard on the radio was always the one that stuck in her head. She had a theory that a woman could always tell what a guy had on his mind by knowing the words to the tune he was humming. Guys' subconscious minds just worked that way. She regarded this as one of the best kept secrets women had; if men were aware women knew this, they would be more guarded about singing in the shower.

Her thoughts changed back to Paula, whose life seemed to have tanked. Anna feared Paula might actually do herself in, just from the e-mail she had sent. Husband in car sales with GM and the Big Three going south, one daughter pregnant at fifteen and the other one having joined a cult and changed her name, bankruptcy looming in the wake of the housing mortgage crisis . . . Paula's list got grittier. But she was saved, Anna thought.

Out of the shower, she toweled off her toned and muscular body as she moved about the apartment. Cold Play cleared her head of Elton John, and she went over to the window to flush the room with spring air. Purple crocuses up next to the brick building across the street caught her eye. The cat came to sit on the window sill and began chittering at some cawing crows.

"You talkin' kitty? Whatcha doin? Git those crows! Git those crows!"

She sometimes thought that if she didn't have the cat to talk to, she might go off the deep end from loneliness. Just then the phone rang, and she picked up to hear a rich male voice in an accent she didn't recognize.

"Miss Washington?"

"Yes?"

"This is Nir Tetzlah calling from the Ein Gedi school for Experiential Education."

"The which? Um, where are you calling from?"

"Israel, Miss Washington, near Jerusalem. Ein Gedi is an oasis plateau in the Judean desert. Very beautiful."

"Ah! Sounds lovely. You must have heard of me from my website." The man's Israeli accent made sense now.

"Yes, I have been looking for organizations like yours . . ."

"Well, I'm not exactly an organization, more like a consultant . . ."

"Yes, yes, that's fine, I understand. But what I am getting at is that we have a school here, an outdoor school, much like your Outward Bound or your National Outdoor Leadership School—only much smaller, of course—and we need both a ropes element course and also a climbing site set up. We think we have found the area we want to use, and although it might be a little . . . um, argued? over . . ."

"Contested?" she interjected.

". . . we need someone to plan it out and make it safe for our students to use within the safety standards of our organization."

"Well, yes, that's what I do. But you understand—my rates are higher than some out there . . ."

"Yes, yes, you shall not worry about that. We have several benefactors who want to see this come into being, and your reputation for precision in the inspection process is very good."

Sounds all right, thought Anna.

"Well, I can't say I speak much Hebrew, although I usually do a crash course before any foreign engagements. When do you want this plotted out? What kind of access does the public have to the area?" she added as an afterthought.

"This is all still under negotiation. The area we are discussing is the Gai ben Hinom valley just outside of the Old City . . . have you been to Israel ever?"

"No. But, uh, I read about it in the news all the time?" she offered.

"Yes, well. We do have that dubious distinction of being a news-making nation. We were thinking not until September or October."

"You know, I have to leave the house right now, but that's a distinct possibility. How can I get back in touch with you?"

Tetzlah gave her the contact number and reminded her of the time difference between Madison and Israel.

She hung up, considering the intriguing proposal. Just then the cat jumped down and started caterwauling, crouching low, as it half crawled, half scooted under the bed. Another tremor was starting—there had been a few lately, only 2–3 on the Richter scale, so slight they were barely noticeable. But the first time it had happened Anna and Jonathan had been in bed, each thinking the other was jiggling a foot. Then Anna noticed the ceiling fan shaking mildly, and said, "Is that you?" "No, I thought it was you," he had replied.

So Anna had called in to the police department. Cold and precise, protecting the peace, they simply ascertained if she had suffered any property damage. When she had said no, they did divulge that several people had called in, and that she should not worry—so long as she hadn't suffered any loss. The whole thing was peculiar, because Wisconsin was not exactly in a fault zone for earthquakes.

Anna looked up at the hanging light in the kitchen as it shook slightly this time. Global warming certainly was having odd and widespread effects.

After she'd run her calloused hands over the cat's soft fur several times, Anna grabbed a cinnamon raisin bagel and gathered up her pack of climbing gear, alarmed the apartment, and took the stairs down two at a time. As she threw the climbing gear into the front passenger seat of the rattletrap Nissan, she groped for her cell phone in her shirt pocket so she could tell Jonathan about this most recent offer for work. She could already see his pursed lips and feel the weight of his silence. He had been trying to persuade her to let go of the out-of-state and overseas work, which took her away for longer than he wanted her to be gone.

"I have a geriatric car, a geriatric laptop, and a geriatric cell phone," she muttered, as she fished out the phone, which had no photo ability and whose owner had no texting ability. "The least they could do is make a fake dial tone," she groused.

For as often as she hated seeing other people using their cell phones when she righteously thought they should be focusing on their driving, she pulled away from the curb, punched in Jonathon's number, and waited for his answer.

"Hey, luv, what's up?" Her heart twinged when she heard his resonant voice, which sounded like it came from old oak caskets that had stored bourbon and been buried under a sunken vessel deep in the ocean.

"Hi! Just finished at the barn, and I'm on my way to the rock gym. Salvatore put up some new routes. Gotta check 'em out."

"Can you call me later in the afternoon?"

"Sounds good. Then I'll tell you about the new offer I just got in today. Pretty exciting, exotic—dangerous, even," she dangled for him.

"Okay sweetie—hold it till later this afternoon. I've got an incoming call."

As they hung up, Anna reflected on how much simpler life was before cell phones, and how much more in touch people had been. Cell phones certainly were useful in a number of ways, but people seemed to turn to obsessively calling one another even in a paradoxically arid landscape of personal contact. Cell phones had to be one of the most ironic technologies for communication in the twentieth century.

Dodging the ubiquitous bicycles of the campus town, she turned the car into what was locally known as the Cow Palace. For a number of years the large domed steel building on the southeastern side of the University of Wisconsin had housed cows for its agricultural program. Then it had been converted into an arena for music performances; a few years ago, a national climbing gym chain based in Baltimore had come in and purchased the building and built one of the premier rock climbing centers in the country. University students populated it, and it became a favorite of families wanting to entertain for their kids' birthday parties, plus get their own kids exercising to combat the flood of obesity that had swept through America with burgers, chips, soda, and lattes. The nation was on a crash course with diabetes and resultant soaring medical costs, so the programs Anna taught were one way the trend was beginning to reverse, she believed.

She parked. Errant apple blossoms wafted on the air, settling like miniature lifeboats on the green sea-lawn. Anna kicked off her Birkenstocks and buried her toes in the grass as she floated towards the climbing center.

Entering, she called out, "Hey Charlie, how you doin'?" to the cleaning guy who was emptying out the paper recycling. Madison's student population offered some diversity, but Wisconsin's midwestern population was mostly white, barring some Hmong immigrants, so Anna always breathed a sigh of relief when she interacted with some real live people of different skin color like Charlie. The brief time she had spent in Baltimore checking out its rock gym she had experienced what it felt like to be a minority, and found it good for her soul.

"I'm arright, Miss Anna, 'n you?"

"Doing better than a poke in the eye with a sharp stick. Any kids' groups coming in today?"

"Them deaf kids due in today. Salvatore laid out some of the ropes upstairs."

"Oh, right, forgot about that. Thanks." She signed in her name and went in to the area with the lockers and toilets, took her harness and friction device out of the pack, and stashed them before heading upstairs to stretch out. She liked the set-up time in the gym because it gave her the chance to reflect, which she often didn't have time for otherwise.

Sal, the climbing specialist from Spain whose parents owned one of the largest rock climbing harness companies in the world, was upstairs laying out ropes and hooking them up to the friction belay devices used for stopping someone's fall. Sal secretly was the envy of every climber there, whether the employees or the regulars, because not only did he have a taut hard body, dark hair, and a delicious accent, but he was independently wealthy, so he could afford to travel the country and the world, designing rock climbing routes in gyms such as this. Whereas Anna liked creating climbing sites outdoors for organizations and schools, Sal preferred mapping out and bolting the specially constructed artificial rock holds people used for hands and feet on walls that were angled and textured with a spray-on concrete surface meant to mimic real outdoors rock. Apart from the occasional lustful eye they threw one another when they were bored or questioning their life choices, Anna and Sal had a high respect for one another and had given each other references often.

"Hey, Sal."

"Hey, Anna." He gave her a wan smile today.

"Sal, were you here just a little while ago? Did you feel that tremor?"

"Fon-kee, eh?" Correct vowel sounds occasionally eluded Sal.

"Yeah. It's just weird. I guess we can't have the rising sea level affect us here like in Bangladesh, but you'd think we've got our share of nature anomalies with the tornadoes and the flooding."

"Where I am from, in Spain, it is very dry now, for several years. We have it in our fields and wells."

"Maybe I'll get there someday."

"No, no, you should go to France, to Chamonix. I cannot believe you have not climbed it."

"Don't rub it in. Someday. Gotta come up with the money, or get a contract from someone over there. Hey, I just got a call to set up a climbing site for an experiential ed school in Israel, near the Dead Sea. Ever climbed in Israel?"

"Israel! Ha! What is there much to climb there, except on the heads of religious people? You be careful if you go over there. That is not a safe place."

"Yeah, well, thanks for your concern. Now all I have to do is tell Jonathon."

"Uh-oh," he clucked at her.

"So we've got the deaf kids today?"

"Si. Remember, they can't just talk when they want to."

Anna nodded her head and laughed. They had an ethical dilemma teaching deaf kids to climb: in order for each kid to learn how to keep his or her peers safe when the climber was attached to the rope and climbing on the wall, the person holding the rope, known as the belayer, had to hold the rope and run it through a friction-creating belay device. Two hands had to be on the rope at all times, and in the event of a climber falling off the wall, the belayer was to crimp down the rope in the belay device so the climber's fall would be arrested.

The trouble with deaf kids learning this was that they communicated with their hands. Usually Anna and Sal heard the soft soundings of deaf people, occasionally growing louder in excitement. But as they grew more excited and wanted to help their climbing partners, or look to an instructor for help, they would take their hands off the rope and begin conversing in American Sign Language. This was not a good thing for the safety of the climber on the rope.

Still, the instructors couldn't exactly tell the belayers they couldn't communicate. So it was a population-specific dilemma. Anna treasured these experiences; they made her a better instructor.

She recalled one of her tensest moments at an outdoor climbing site teaching a deaf kid, Aaron, to rappel. Rappelling was a counterintuitive activity that consisted of hooking a person up to a rope and telling him to walk backward off a cliff. One kid had actually vomited before going over the edge because he couldn't bring himself to defy his elders and say "No! I won't!" With Aaron, Anna had a safety rope on him for backup, and he was supposed to control his own rate of descent with the same friction device climbers used for climbing up rock. He began whimpering,

"OhbyGot, OhbyGot," his m's voiced as b's. His hands flailed, speaking what, she could only guess. Once she had convinced him to get his hands back on the rope and his face had changed back from ashen to pink, she had called the interpreter up and the two of them had successfully talked him backwards off the sixty-foot cliff.

Sal belayed Anna up the test routes, watching the well-toned latissimus dorsi muscles work in her back. She checked to make sure all of the holds were bolted in securely, no "spinners," which could disconcert a climber at best, and at worst make him peel off the wall unexpectedly, usually getting scraped or banged up in the process.

"So when would this be? You going to Israel." He lowered her off the climb.

"Probably not till the fall."

"And you're just here for the summer, teaching classes and working at the barn?"

"Yeah, some, and I'll be writing the sports rag for the U."

Between the rock climbing work and the riding lessons she taught at a stable dedicated to saving mustangs, Anna did well enough financially, but her family felt she underutilized her potential—meaning, she was too smart for what she was doing. She should have gone to Princeton for law. Jonathan saw the logic in this, and was generally on her family's side, which didn't sit well with her.

Jonathan wanted to marry Anna—he said. She resisted on a couple of counts. First, she wanted more from Jonathan. He made a good living, but guts to accompany the heart on his sleeve would have suited her better. He was reserved with his emotions—blocked, even, at times. Going into a relationship most women would think they could change this quality in a man, but instead Anna just observed.

Resistance came naturally to Anna, but her consistent refusal of Jonathan had more to do with evasion than obstinacy. While she could see herself being a mother, she couldn't see herself being a wife. She had nieces and nephews she adored; she would have been loving, and an adequate disciplinarian. She knew how to keep someone safe. She could see herself being in charge of a relationship, such as mothering, or teaching a class, but she couldn't picture herself surrendering to one. Jonathan compared her to a wrestler with all the right slippery moves. At least Jonathan was a good climbing partner.

Beyond what she intuited about the relationship she was in, Anna was hardly familiar with her deeper beliefs. She thought the popularization of Buddhism in America was a wonderful guideline for living, and was curious about Taoism, and what on earth all those people in China might believe; she admired some "New Age" concepts, or the metaphors for life presented by quantum mechanics; but she kept her nose focused very much in the culture of the present, even though technologically she was somewhat handicapped.

Her work-related travels to other countries were curios, dolls in local traditional costume collected and put in the closet of her mind. Had she been called on for any serious commitment or conviction of belief, she would have politely dodged the request. Philosophical arguments over beer held no attraction for her.

The notion of going to where people died daily for their beliefs in a land that had been fraught with strife and soaked in blood for millennia began to irritate her; she wasn't capable of comprehending how seriously the inhabitants took religion. She supposed she should ask her friend Paula for some tips about the area, since the woman had made a couple of trips to the "Holy Land," but she'd have to let some time pass before she sent out an e-mail. She was sick of the drama from that sector.

Sal lowered her down out of her reverie.

"All set then?"

"Looks good to me. Bring 'em on."

She rehearsed in her head how the climbing lesson would go, but got stuck when she tried to apply the same technique to telling Jonathon that night that she intended to go to Israel in the fall.

6

Capernaum

SABBATH WAS IMMINENT. RIVKA underwent so much preparation for the day of rest, even with Aviel's and Devorah's help, that she thought it no wonder Adonai rested on the seventh day—He must have been exhausted. Especially without a woman to help him do the work. She knew that when scripture said that everyone in a man's house was to rest on the Sabbath, including his slaves and ass and so on, the fact that his wife had been left out of the exemption from labor simply meant that she and her husband were a unit; there was no need to mention her as an individual. Nonetheless, she thought it an irony that it was the woman who did all the work in preparation and she was not, in fact, able to rest on the Sabbath. Somebody had to clean the dishes after the meal. In the beginning she had complained to Jairus but realized she was only creating a lack of rest for both of them by doing so, so with time she relented and her tongue grew less sharp. The ever-so-slight smoothing of her husband's brow was the only indication that she had found the way to create *shalom bayit*, peace in the household.

Jairus had declined having servants or slaves, even though they could have afforded them. So, when it came to tasks ranging from large to small, whether slaughtering, or making bread, or tidying the house, or carrying water buckets for the animals, all of this had to be done in advance by the family in order to uphold the prohibition of doing any work on the Sabbath. If they had had a non-Jewish slave, he or she could have done the work for them—but Jairus didn't like the idea. He had Greek notions that all people were more or less equal, and he could not bring himself to order around anyone. Fortunately, that meant he did not dictate to his wife or children, either. He was a benevolent, in fact, indulgent, head of the household.

Rivka heaved the goat's milk bucket in her calloused hand. She had heard of wealthy women in Jerusalem dipping their hands in a special wax to soften their skin, then having their nails trimmed and shaped.

What loveliness! she sighed. But then she corralled her momentarily extravagant thoughts, grateful that her daughter was alive and that she was bringing in milk rather than her daughter's funeral linens.

It should be a special Sabbath because of their joy, but right now it was not going so well. Aviel seemed to have lost her balance in the order of the household and was having difficulty regulating her mood. When she wasn't doing her chores obstinately, she would go into the corner of the room she shared with Devorah, and look out on the yard with the goats and the mule. She was writing furiously, her hair strewn wild and loose about her shoulders, her bare feet tucked awkwardly under her with no regard for decorum as she sat hunched and scribbling.

On this Sabbath Devorah interrupted her in one such moment. Devorah was more lithe than her sister, and three years younger. Because the younger had already started her cycle, Aviel sometimes felt she was the second child, but Devorah did not think any less of her sister. She was still a little too young to comprehend the change that had gone on internally for Aviel these last few days; she was simply glad she still had her sister with her.

"What are you writing now?" Devorah asked as she brushed past Aviel and glanced at the papyrus.

"I want to get out. I want to get out of here. I can barely look at people. You know I've wanted to go to a bigger city before this. Maybe Ephesus. Maybe Jerusalem. I need to get away from people's scrutiny. There is no privacy in this tiny bowl of a town," Aviel growled over her shoulder.

"Aviel! Did Yeshua make you mad? How would you live? Who would you live with, and what would you do?"

"Aunt Miriam and Uncle Mordechai. You know they would take me in. Oh, Devorah, you could come and live there with me too . . ." she turned to her sister with a desperate look, as if she would pack her things and leave that afternoon.

"Aviel! What about *Eemah* and *Abba*? How would they survive? They need us! Surely it's not so bad for you here—people care about you, that's all. They just don't know how to respond. And Daniel, maybe even Nathan, are interested in you . . ."

Aviel snorted and turned back to the papyrus. She crumpled it and swept it off the writing table with her hand, then put her head in her hands. She wanted Devorah to understand, not challenge her now.

"Devorah, you mean well, but you are still young as far it goes in knowing about men. Daniel is a good man, but he is my boyhood friend. And Nathan . . . Nathan is a snake. Just give me a little time to myself, please," she grumbled.

Devorah could see that her words could give no solace, so she came over to her sister and gently stroked her forehead and hair a few times, then left the room.

As Sabbath grew closer, the ethereal peace that regularly descended on the town continued to elude the household. Aviel's temper again flared at her father in the close quarters later that Friday afternoon.

"I should have died! Instead I am an object of healing!" Aviel cried at her father with as much fire as she could manage, still drained from her illness. He had asked her what was troubling her. "It makes absolutely no difference how I'm supposed to respond to this, this . . . miracle," she spat out at him as her hands flailed in the air. "All that mattered to Yeshua is that you believe he is the messiah. I have been used to prove something to you: that he is a divinely inspired healer. And now you are complaining how this complicates your life at the synagogue. Why do I care how difficult it's made it for you? Has it occurred to you how I might be affected? I should have died and been in peace by now!" Jairus was uncertain as to what he had said that had provoked her.

Overhearing in the next room, Rivka winced as she busied herself, thinking perhaps she had taught her daughter to loose her tongue just a little too much. What man would have such a girl?

Aviel stormed out of the house in tears, stopping only to touch her hand automatically to the doorway's mezuzah, which contained a miniature scroll of the Shema, the profession of faith every Jew knew by heart. It was the commandment to love Adonai, the One God, with all of one's heart and soul. She touched her fingers to her lips, picked up her skirts, and fled.

Jairus moved to the doorway while his eyes followed his beloved daughter. At least she was feeling better, he thought ruefully. As he watched her march toward the olive groves, he contemplated what to do with her next.

"I think she is upset with me," he remarked to his wife as she glided into the room and sighed. She put her hand on her husband's shoulder.

"Let her go off. Maybe she'll find some of the answers that she's been looking for in her heart instead of her head."

It was true: the town's talk after Yeshua's visit had been so intense that Jairus had made himself scarce from the synagogue for a few days, as if recovering with his daughter. When Aviel had questioned him about his staying at home, telling him she was fine and he could return to his normal duties, he admitted to her that he didn't know how to explain to the elders what had happened. He was uncomfortable under his skin; he didn't want to have to answer for having sought out Yeshua. Seeking out a miracle worker in and of itself was not such an unusual act, but Yeshua's message about the imminent kingdom of God, along with the healings he'd done, had spread as all the most dramatic bits of human information do—as if people had nothing else occupying their lives but gossip.

Even Yohanon had questioned Jairus, though discreetly, not wanting to press. Old as he was, Yohanon had seen miracle workers before, but none so bizarrely graphic in their results. Usually in a healing ritual there were a lot of words and performances that seemed to be directed to the gawkers, most of them children, and of course the affected grieving parties. Usually, the healers wanted to be paid. With Yeshua, it was as if everything in the matter was turned upside down completely, him coming in amongst ridicule, violating cleanliness laws, leaving more quietly than he had come, and with a resurrection, no less. He had said Aviel wasn't dead, just sleeping. But what did he mean by sleep? That could be interpreted in so many different ways.

So Yohanon had changed the subject quickly, simply expressing gratitude that Aviel was well. He asked Jairus for the final payment on the scribal table and tools, and Jairus had paid up. Jairus thought Yohanon should present the table to Aviel personally, and Yohanon was grateful for this recognition of the girl's specialness to him. Now, he was simply waiting for the right moment to give it to her.

Aviel muttered to herself as she strode up the sloped hill behind the village's houses and marketplace, which smelled of fresh fish, gesticulating with her hand. At times the burning in it was reduced to a tingling, but it was never quiet, except, it occurred to her now, when she wrote. Perhaps she could write more and see if the sensation went and stayed away. She had mentioned the hand to her parents, but they were at a loss about it.

"Fine. An entire village turned on its ear. People peer at me oddly because I am alive when I should be dead—but it's not about my life. Who knows how far and wide this story will carry? And yet it's the man,

Yeshua, about whom they'll talk. He builds his reputation on my life. In my own place, my own home, I'm like garbage that gets tossed out and burned in outer Gehenna because everyone is scared of me now. Well, at least since no one knows me beyond these confines, it is the miracle on which people will focus around the region. But that makes me the scraps for the goat! I should go away. I didn't ask for this!" she shouted, kicked the dirt, and looked up at the sky, wringing her hands as if she could throw away from her the very air. As she began crying again she pounded the burning hand into her chest repeatedly.

A truant sheepdog ran up beside her and sniffed at her skirts, circling about her like a Hebrew bride circling her husband in a marriage ceremony. "I don't want you, beast." She aimed her foot at it but kept walking through the olive groves and past a gathering of oil presses. Finally acquiescing to the dog's presence when it wasn't deterred, she began talking to it as it fell in alongside her.

"I'm a freak. A freak of nature. Who would have me now, even if I did want to marry—which I don't," she grudged at the mottled dog. "Is it such a terrible thing for a girl, a woman, whatever I am, to want to move my body, or to create through the power of the word rather than through the power of the flesh? Words last longer than flesh—a lot longer, if they are preserved properly," she said, thinking of the ancient and mysteriously scripted Egyptian papyrus some of the Bedouin traders had shown when they had come through on their routes. "That's all I want to do. Is write. I don't want a husband. I am content with the family I have."

Her parents couldn't keep her inside, they knew that, but she couldn't be a shepherd outside. She couldn't quite explain why she was so angry at her father, but in the last few days since she had come back from death, she knew her life had taken on a quality she could not express to her parents. At least Devorah, her sister, seemed a little closer to understanding. She didn't resist Aviel's description of her peaceful death state, but her parents seemed afraid to hear about it. Her heart searched for the phrases to explain, but her mother and her father couldn't touch upon it with her. Their daughter's eyes had acquired an even greater depth with her blood knowledge, a depth beyond them. She was absent now of that lurking fear of death that crept up behind humankind leaning towards its last days.

Woman and dog stopped. She sat down at the base of a fig tree mixed in with the olives, and felt the binding of the under-linens that her mother had wrapped and bandaged her in, just to make sure there was no more bleeding as she healed. The old dog sighed and circled several times, then curled into a warm comforting patch of fur. Aviel caressed the dog as she sat and looked up at the sky that built promisingly toward rain clouds. She kneaded the meeting place of the dog's shoulder and haunch, calming herself. Like the dog, she decided, she was not sure how many times or why she needed to circle before lying down, but she was doing just that, circling, circling in her mind. She was fairly certain she wouldn't remain in Capernaum. Maybe the ostracism that had accompanied the miracle would work in her favor.

From under her tunic Aviel pulled out a small leather book with the finest of thin papyrus pages bound together. Then she unwrapped from a cotton wad a reed stylus and a small clay pot of ink sealed with wax. Cracking open the seal, she dipped the stylus in the ink and began to write in miniature Hebrew letters. The writing absorbed her thoroughly as the paper drank the ink, and her anger fled like black crows to the pastures' far reaches. For now she was joined with the breeze and songbirds and the stylus scratching on the papyrus. She had begun a practice of reflection in writing that she would keep the remainder of her life. As she wrote, her heart stilled.

Her hand tilted into the writing implement as she scrawled the tiny letters across the sheet from right to left. The papyrus, sent from her educated Aunt Miriam in Jerusalem, was so finely finished that she was able to write in an unusual way: on both sides of the papyrus. This way, she could get down twice as many words in the small leather notebook. There were no spaces between the individual words; it struck her at one point that the flow of the letters together, after the manner of the day, was like the relationships of her life, with little or no space between the characters, and no punctuation. So, in reality, the text read more like *SurelyJohnsmiss ionlieswithYeshuanotwithawoman.* As she wrote she relinquished concern for grammar and wrote directly from the deeper recesses of her mind and heart. These words were private, intended for no one. Finally, she had her privacy. It occurred to her that she would rather sacrifice writing than let what she wrote be seen by anyone.

After writing for what must have been close to an hour, she blew on the last of the ink, closed the notebook, and tucked it back into her clothing again. "I think I'll join you in a nap," Aviel said to the dog, feeling more peaceful. She slid farther down onto the grass and put her head on the balled-up wad of fur, which grunted and licked its nose, let out an "oomph," then fell back asleep.

In her dream she sank down into a swirling backdrop that held the man John in folds of brown fabric. He emerged from behind the folds and put large arms around her in an enveloping caress so that she felt utterly warm and safe.

She awoke as the sun would have been nearing the horizon, though clouds covered it as they gathered in a dark and threatening bolus off over the lake. Her head was on the ground because the dog had gotten up and left. Grass that she brushed out of her hair rose up in spirals, scattering on the wind. The hairs on the back of her neck began to tingle, so she turned to her left and looked into the olive groves, their dull green leaves twirling on short stems in the gathering wind. Then, she knotted into a crouch, crimping her skirts close about her.

Nathan was leaned up against a tree several lengths away, and while she couldn't see his eyes clearly she knew he was looking at her as he rapidly stroked himself, naked, in a kneeling position. Aviel scrambled to a couple of trees farther away and hid behind one with a thick and sturdy trunk. Panting, she pressed her back into it. Her hands shook and she started crying, but she bit her lip, spun from behind the tree, and drove towards Nathan. Abruptly stopping his obscene motion as she drew near, he scrabbled in the dirt for his tunic and tried to duck behind his tree.

She stamped up to him. Her writing hand stiffened, rose, and pointed into his face. Years of trust from their childhood play dissolved in the bile rising into her throat.

A flush of spreading shame pulled up his slack lower lip, and he wiped spittle from his mouth with the back of his hand. Yet the intrusion pushed forward in her mind. She spat and kicked duff at him, as he groveled backward on his knees in the dirt.

"What? Aviel! I didn't do anything! Aviel! What's wrong?"

"You will regret this." Aviel collected her rage and her skirts and turned her back to him. Running off, she startled a flock of crows that cawed in chorus as she fled for home.

7

AVIEL HALF RAN, HALF walked back to the town, wiping her arm across her face and nose as she went. The grass rattled rather than whispered now as the wind built as the clouds began to wring out rain. She stopped at a twisted olive tree and leaned up against it. Tears came out of her as blood had so recently, and with them washed her rage at Nathan's violation and indignity. She had got away from the scene in the moment, but the image dogged her. As the flood of emotion moved through her and found its natural crescendo then decline, she began to think more clearly. Yet she felt a desperation: how could she escape the effects of such an effrontery? She lived in a tightly bound society.

She walked now, rain running in rivulets down her legs. As she came up her street she saw Yohanon pulling in his work table. At least this kind man had remained solicitous of her welfare, at least he had not pried in the wake of the miracle, she consoled herself. He respected her dignity.

Her hair soaking, she raced into the house without the automatic touch to the mezuzah. She had left the house crying, and came back in crying, but this time the show of emotion was quieter. Jairus knew something was wrong when her saw her. She plopped down on the bed, her shoulders heaving. Coming to her, her father put an arm around her. As if he were contaminated, being a man, she shrank from him, but he pressed through her anger and held her in close.

"What's wrong, honey? What happened?"

She recounted the sordid experience, and Jairus felt rage rise in his throat, felt his legs tighten in anger. "I will . . ." the unfleshed-out threat hung in the air, more ominous in its vagueness.

"*Abba*, don't do anything. I took care of it. He'd only deny it; there was no one else there to witness," except the dog, she added to herself. But then, maybe that was why the dog had run off before she woke.

Jairus raised his eyes to the ceiling and cursed silently. He knew if he applied the laws for protection of his daughter the process would get ugly. There was already enough controversy around her.

"I want to go away, *Abba*," Aviel dropped on him.

"Away?"

"To Jerusalem. I have enough knowledge now to be a scribe. I can work and send money back to you and *Eemah*. I can't stay here. I can't stay here now with this happening, this thing with Nathan, and with what Yeshua has done. How can I stay? You'd think I'm unclean, the way people treat me. They can only treat well what and who they understand." She hung her head.

Jairus picked her chin up with a finger that still shook with residual anger.

"You are clean, daughter. You have nothing to be ashamed of. You cleansed yourself in the waters of the *mikvah*. Adonai has forgiven you. Yeshua knew that; that's why he told you to do the cleansing. He wanted to be sure! He did care for you as best he could."

"Why are you defending him?"

"We owe your life to him! He came when I asked. Do you understand the status he has, the things he's been doing?"

"I don't care about him!" she was on the verge of tears again. "Who is he to me? Yes, I'm grateful he saved my life, but he left me to piece it back together myself. He left. I live here. What am I supposed to do now? I'm still not a woman. Am I supposed to just fit back in to the ordinary conduct of life here?"

"You know you are not alone in this. *Eemah* and I will help. Devorah is here for you."

"I want to go away. You know I'll be fine," she pressed.

"And live where? With whom? You're unmarried!" he raised his voice in frustration.

The downpour continued outside, and Rivka came dashing into the house. She saw her daughter and husband in close talk and decided to give them privacy as she went to change out of her soaked clothing.

"Aunt Miriam and Uncle Mordechai?" Aviel posed the option to her father. "They might have use for me, preparing bills of sale, keeping accounts, writing correspondence, copying books. My uncle will have connections and can supervise my learning."

"You're presuming a lot!" He twisted partially away from her and worked his hands on the fabric on his legs.

"But it's a possibility, isn't it?" She jumped on his not having said no automatically.

Jairus knew he was sunk. It was yet another thing to present to Rivka, whose first response would be fear at this proposal. Still, he hoped in the knowledge that she must have known it would come at some point, Aviel being so interested in writing. Going to the larger city made most sense if she were to pursue the path. Jairus just hadn't thought it would come so soon. He sat still, very still, as he looked again at his beloved daughter.

"You know I would do anything for your happiness. I know you have a gift. I just think it's too early; you're too young. And you're still healing."

"I've just been through the valley of death and back and you think I'm too inexperienced to handle the city of Jerusalem?"

He turned his palms up on his thighs, looking helplessly at his hands.

"I will strangle Nathan myself."

"*Abba.*" Her face reflected distaste. "I took care of it. Something in equal measure will happen to him. The world works this way, I know, even at my age. You don't have to lift a finger. Let it go. God will punish him."

Jairus cried at the thought that his daughter had been so miraculously retrieved, only to suffer such a lurid betrayal at the hands of the world. To escape both, she was proposing to go to a place that only offered more of the same, he was convinced; his fear was enough for both him and his wife.

"How will *Eemah* allow it?" he spoke as if to himself.

"You know, *Eemah* has told me 'from your mouth to God's ears' all my life, and she knows what my hopes are, what I have wished. But she'll need help with the house. It's too much for *Eemah* and Devorah alone. You should get a servant. I wish you'd consider it. And I wish *Eemah* didn't have to know about Nathan."

"What about Nathan?" Rivka echoed as she came into the room.

Jairus looked at Aviel. As Aviel relented and told her the story, her mother's lips pursed and her eyes narrowed. She sat down, stock still, on the bench by the wall. Aviel told her how she had threatened the shepherd, and Rivka nodded in approval, not just at her daughter's particular choice of words, but also knowing a woman's resources in such a situation were severely limited. She flirted in her mind with the idea of going to some of the old women who knew of pagan practices, so she could curse Nathan, but she banished the thought and composed her face before her husband.

"So I want to go away to Jerusalem, *Eemah*," said Aviel. "I have just told *Abba* why: to live with Aunt Miriam and become a scribe, to be relieved of this—this baking oven I live in here."

Her mother was quiet for a few moments. She was like so many other mothers, who had significant intelligence but nothing to push their minds against, so that the energy they would have used for creative ideas in the external world they took and used to manipulate the relationships in their lives. In this fashion Rivka had hooked herself to her family more through power than love. Still, she recognized when she should stop rearranging her husband's and daughters' lives like a bouquet to keep herself stimulated. Getting up and coming over to her daughter, she put her hands on Aviel's head and hair, and kissed her on the top of the head. Rivka's constrained expressions of fondness were often a mystery to her family. Without comment she left the room and went in the back to mix and knead bread while she thought.

"Well. We will think about it," Jairus surmised from his wife's behavior. "We would have to write your aunt. And you need to get your new scribal table from Yohanon," he remembered.

The rain had not kept away their Sabbath guests, so Yohanon and Hepsabah, and David and Ruth, a childless younger couple from the synagogue, came in through the doorway that evening after the scripture had been read. Ruth, a delicate and fine-boned young girl with large eyes disproportionate to her features, looked sidelong at Aviel, wondering about Yeshua's actions, too polite to ask directly. David, clearly besotted with his wife despite her lack of producing children, cleared his throat a number of times looking back and forth between Ruth and Aviel as if he couldn't quite grasp the difference between them; they were both females. The undercurrent of the dinner celebration was quiet, and Devorah cleaned up after they had all left arm in arm, walking back on the blessedly mud-covered streets to their own homes.

In bed, Rivka and Jairus discussed their daughters in the intimate, conspiratorial after-hours hush that parents do, observing, worrying, criticizing, hoping, planning a trajectory far beyond the reaches they had ever planned for themselves, yet with trepidation, fearing they would be surpassed as they saw their own youthfulness running to the shadows of age.

"I'll send word with the next caravan going to Jerusalem. I hope Miriam will welcome this. She certainly doesn't owe me anything, after *Eemah* died," Rivka said, referring to her sister's care of their mother in her last crabbed years in the big city. The old woman had barely survived the trip from Capernaum to Jerusalem, and had never comfortably adjusted to the city. Towards the end, she had lost her mind as well as her bowels, on a regular basis, and Miriam would write Rivka describing the horrific, foul-smelling job to which she was reduced. Their mother had been sharp-witted and proud, too proud, and she had wrapped Miriam and Rivka's father around her thumb. But he had died too early for his time, and she had gradually loosened all the controls on her daughters, her thoughts, even her bodily functions. Miriam and Rivka thought it ironic, and Rivka still felt indebted to Miriam for the strain she had suffered during their mother's decline. Rivka hoped that Aviel's going to live with her aunt might be a help, a recompense in some sense.

"Our daughter has a great skill; she'll be very useful. Perhaps Mordechai can place her well, and there are more men there for her anyway—better men than we seem to be able to offer here," Jairus said with disgust in his voice.

"The next thing you know, Devorah will be wanting to go, though, and I need her here still."

"I'll hire someone for you, to help with the work—will you agree?"

"Help with the spinning and washing and feeding the livestock and butchering and cooking . . ." she reeled off the list of chores, thumping each one, reminding him how much work she was responsible for.

"Yes, yes, all that and more," he rolled his eyes, and drew himself on top of her, pinning her.

"Careful, you don't want to flatten the lady of the household," she laughed, and the stresses of recent days floated off on a tide of caress and sensation.

"Impossible!" he retorted.

After, they cocooned, Jairus snoring softly as the household slumbered.

Word came back in a relatively short amount of time that Miriam and Mordechai would be delighted to have Aviel; in fact, the timing was quite good for their quiet household.

Aviel went to collect the scribal table from Yohanon on a brilliant and crisp day. He sat, as usual, at the front of his house, his back to the stone, this day working with soft cedar making a miniature toy donkey. Just down the street Devorah and a young boy named Mattan were poking at an insect in the dirt, the happiness of childhood floating around them.

"So, you're leaving us to go to the big city, the holy place. You'll never want to come back; we're so simple here by comparison."

"Have you been to Jerusalem, Yohanon?"

"Oh yes, many years ago, on a pilgrimage," and he pushed his chin into the air, remembering the smells and sights. "It's the shining city, the most holy place I've ever been. You'll be amazed. But spoiled, too, by all the luxuries. And the priests are compromised having to satisfy both Rome's laws and our laws. Write me a letter and let me know what you see."

"I'll write large, so you can read what I have to say."

"Good. Excellent. Now, I have known you since you were no bigger than a gourd, and I know you'll do with those hands something no one else has done. You'll see. And I will say 'I knew her when she was this high,'" as his gnarled hands gestured a foot and a half up from the dirt.

She came up close and knelt down before him. He smiled upon her, got up and went inside, and came back out with the table and a stylus.

"Let me know how this one fits, how it serves you. I will always make for you what you need. God willing."

The scribe, not yet a woman, no longer a girl, took the table from him, somber-faced, her hand tingling more as she received the gift.

"Thank you, my dear friend. I will use it and remember you."

As she was turning down the street to make final preparations for Jerusalem, Aviel looked back once at Yohanon, but he did not look up to watch her go. He simply continued to carve the piece of cedar, feeling the dull ache of loss once again.

8

Madison

Jonathan Cohen sat back in his chair on the porch overlooking Lake Mendota, one of two twin lakes in Madison, and chewed his pencil as Anna told him about her offer. He sighed. The lake had whitecaps today, and only a few bold sailboats skipped about. Ruefully he recalled the time he'd had to be rescued by the university boat patrol because he couldn't get his sailboard back to the dock the day he'd been learning. Then Anna's words washed over him and he forced himself back to paying attention.

". . . and I wondered if you'd want to come with me, since you know the place, even though it's been a while since you've been there . . ."

The curl of the waves splashing on the rocks that lined his lawn and dock reminded Jonathan of the curve of the small of Anna's back, the part that just started up onto her hip—

"Are you listening?"

"Yeah, um, it sounds like a good opportunity for you," and his mind reluctantly returned to the conversation. "But how long did you say you'd be gone?" He smelled the pencil wood and looked at his chew marks.

"Well that's just it. About three, maybe four weeks, but if you came with me, you could come maybe part of the time, like I was saying. Are you listening?"

"Yes, I'm listening. Quit asking me that." He frowned and ran his fingers through his dark wavy hair, then flipped forward in the calendar he had at his desk. His broad shoulders hunched. "It's too busy a time of year for me. We've got a large contract for a thirty-thousand-square-foot house up in Door County—don't ask me why people need so much space, and check it out, they have eleven bathrooms—I just can't hand it over to the guys and take off. You should see the plans for the cabinets these people want. Acacia wood. Guess they aren't affected by the recession." Jonathan had moved from being a woodworker for a kitchen cabinet company to starting up his own business in upscale furniture design.

"Oh." Anna sounded slightly put out, but not to the degree that Jonathan would have liked. "Well, then, maybe you could just help me with some of the Hebrew before I go." She paused. "Look, hon, I know you're tired of me going off for these gigs, but it's my breath, my lifeblood. I feel needed. I have an expertise, and I'm good at this, and I get paid well. It's not like we're married with kids and I'm abandoning them and you. And besides, it's Israel, and you should understand the excitement of that."

"Israel's a mess these days."

"When has Israel not been a mess?"

He tossed the pencil toward the wastebasket. "Yeah, okay, whatever."

But Anna knew he wasn't happy, and she was at a loss as to how to soothe him about it. She perceived Jonathan to be like the rock for her: immovable. She was aware at a certain level that her family history led her to desire someone who would unflinchingly be there for her. Yet she was beginning to realize she wanted solidity, but not rock-hard immovability. She needed more bending.

Anna was able to give to people who needed special and extra attention, or to psychologically impaired horses, but when it came to the personal relationships in her life, she wanted them in neater packages. Jonathan was about as self-sufficient as a grown man could get, but she did realize she asked him to spend more time on his own than most other intimate relationships would have asked.

For his part, Jonathan was a good man, a mensch. He could understand there were several aspects of his personality that were not the easiest to deal with: his temper, and sometimes his ego, which Anna told him was like that of most men-boys who needed to have a woman/mother figure look in their direction to give witness to the fact that they were Doing Something. There was also the annoying quirk that he didn't seem to see his socks after he'd left them on the floor, as if he were expecting Godzilla to come crashing through the door at any moment and that took all his attention. But all in all, he thought he was a pretty good snag for her, and he tired of her scuttling away from his attempts to draw them closer together. He had been infinitely patient with her. Maybe too patient—sometimes he thought he should be more assertive, simply tell her, look, it's me or the trips. But so far he hadn't brought himself to do it.

More trips meant more distance. He just didn't seem able to find the route around Anna's reticence to draw her closer. Even after they'd been intimate she'd back off, as if the stove was too hot. She seemed to have a need to run, to stay itinerant, unattached, even while she had a strong need to be needed, almost as strong as his. They had talked about trust a few times, but not in great depth. And in the end, he didn't think talking would make the difference. Intuitively he sensed her heart needed to change in some way towards him.

He sighed despondently and said, "Look, you know I'm ambivalent about Israel and the whole Jewish thing, anyway. You go. You can learn Hebrew just fine if you sign up for a class taught in a conversion course at Congregation Beth El. I'm sure they have them rotating pretty regularly since it's such a large congregation."

Raised a Conservative Jew, Jonathan had fled his roots ever since his father, the cantor for a large New Jersey synagogue, had blown apart the family with an affair that Jonathan's mother could not claw her way back up and over. Jonathan and his sister had been seventeen and thirteen respectively at the time. The family was spared public shame because his father had resigned his position and taken a year off before moving to Minnesota and taking a job at a small synagogue, but the family imploded. There were myths about Jewish families, such as that domestic violence did not happen in Jewish families, so a synagogue official's affair shocked the community as violently as did Catholic priests who abused young boys.

Jonathan didn't like the idea of visiting Israel even in his mind. The trip he had taken there when he was sixteen was colored retrospectively by knowing now that his father had been at the height of his infidelity with the blonde legal secretary who, thankfully, was not a member of the synagogue, not even Jewish. Jonathan supposed she was exotic to his father, who had grown up in Lithuania and whose parents had been concentration camp survivors.

The greatest devastation of Jonathan's own life, besides seeing his mother's eyes trying to contain a pain too deep for a human soul, was that he had only sporadic and strained contact with his sister. So he very much wanted Anna to be family for him.

Anna was the delight of his life—her deep laughter, her athletic body, the way she responded to him, and how she would listen when they talked late at night on the porch, listening to the waves lap the shore, or the owl hooting in the dark cover of woods.

It wasn't important to him that Anna convert to Judaism; it wasn't even so important that they have children. But he did very much want to make her his wife. Her traveling lodged a barrier between them. Yet sometimes he wondered if the trips were just a physical manifestation of a more metaphoric divide. It was as if it were a shield for her, a wall she raised almost every time they began getting closer.

Anna was the smartest person he knew, and that was saying a lot, since he held the silent and (he felt) benign prejudice that Jews were smarter than the broader population, intelligent "in the best sort of way," he would say to her. She wasn't just smart thinking-wise, but emotionally and intuitively as well, at an ineffable level. She engaged him. She was never boring.

"Look, let's just let it go for now. Come for dinner. We'll walk the neighborhood after," Jonathan offered.

"Around six?"

"See you then."

"It always strikes me as a little odd that you eat ham, even though I know it doesn't matter to you so much," Anna commented on Jonathan's good midwestern choice of glazed ham for dinner with home made mashed potatoes.

"What? Why? Even really good Jews stray a little. My grandfather, who was a rabbi, said he was sure God must have made a mistake about lobster not being kosher. Which means that my grandfather ate lobster at some point. He didn't get struck by a lightning bolt that I know of."

Anna laughed and shook her head and they played their like-married-people-but-not-really routine as they set the table together and watched the evening news.

Later in the evening, after they'd finished a bottle of Mirrasou cabernet, Anna walked out the sliding glass doors barefoot in the grass to watch the sun set over the lake. Green growth and the tannin from trees that colored midwestern waters brown wafted on the warm lake air. Jonathan came out and picked a yellow Johnny jump-up and presented it to Anna. She smiled, and they clasped hands and stood silently considering the end of another day, when there seemed to be so many in a summer rush of lawn sprinklers and fireworks and sailboats.

"Ice cream?" he asked.

"Sure. I'll get Maisley and we can chase down the jingle-jangle ice cream man."

Maisley was Jonathan's still bouncy but aging Scottish terrier, who delighted in walks through the neighborhood. An invisible electric fence in the backyard allowed her to run free and threaten the squirrels in the morning, sniffing at the lake and generally keeping a keen eye on the neighbors' comings and goings, but evening was her favorite time because she had Jonathan's full attention, and she could wander on the retracting leash.

As they padded the cooling cement sidewalk sprouting weeds in every crack, Anna looped her arm through Jonathan's, feeling the dog tugging slightly on the other end of the leash. The dog sniffed everything: tonight it was magisterial elms that had escaped the Dutch elm disease that had ravaged the Midwest in the latter half of the century. A tinny Scott Joplin tune alerted them to nutty buddies and popsicles, for which they shelled out change like trading marbles for the cooling treats, which they shared with Maisley. The deepening twilight, their contented stomachs, and their silence cozied them into one another. When they returned after the dog's approval of all things normal in the neighborhood, they put aside their daily cares of work and the future of their relationship, then knew it was time to move towards the bedroom.

Hands on her hips, Jonathan drew Anna close into his pelvis, looking first into her eyes to find her consent, then next at the hair on the top of her head as he fused their torsos. They moved as a unit, he backwards, she shuffling her feet forward with his. He yielded up one hand and caressed her hair, then began kissing her ear. She turned her lips into his neck, and like taffy peeling away from his chest, kept the connection through her kisses on his skin as she opened his shirt. Jonathan bumped into the bed and they fell backwards onto it, laughing and rolling about.

Somehow she knew, just moments before he experienced it, the spiral winding of their energies upward as his life flowed into her. She smiled wanly at him, and he collapsed on her, his body damp but not heavy for her. Peace enveloped them. Then he slept, and she drifted off with him.

9

Two days later, Anna and Sal headed northwest out of Madison towards Devil's Lake, on a day of woolly sheep clouds speckling blue sky. They were going to set some ropes on a few climbs for a clinic later in the morning.

"How did Jonathan take your going to Israel?" Sal figured he knew Anna well enough by now to ask.

"Lukewarm." She seemed not to want to stay on the subject so switched it by asking, "Hey, d'you hear the Dalai Lama's coming to town?"

"Dolly, Schmolly. Why should I think of this guy as His Holiness? That's what I saw on a brochure one time. Holy to whom?" He was okay with changing the subject from Jonathan, who couldn't get out of his own way, as far as Sal could see. The guy was a decent climber, but someone like Anna would need a more commanding partner than her current boyfriend, he thought.

"He's pretty with it, you know," said Anna reflecting on the Tibetan leader. "He's into science, and the idea that how we think about our lives influences them. Negatively or positively. The guy's really smart, in addition to being a brilliant political refugee. I think I'll go hear him speak.'

"You know, Anna, I was raised Catholic. It's the marrow of my bones, where I come from. My parents tried to get me more interested in it, it didn't work, and then those idiot priests came along and made it embarrassing to even think of myself as Catholic. I don't have much use for religion."

"Well, I can't argue with what your upbringing was like," Anna reflected. "I don't buy the patriarchal power structure of Catholicism, but there's something beautifully ancient about the faith. Faith. I tried Unitarianism for a while, but it just seemed so head-oriented to me, and not enough God in it. At least you had a religious upbringing. I had a great-great-grandfather who was a Baptist preacher out in Oregon in the 1800s, had a PhD and all, but the rest of the family disowned him I guess. My parents didn't bring me up anything. I suppose the rock is my church."

Sal took this in, respecting the fact that Anna had made any mention of her family, which she virtually never did.

The car drove out past defunct grain storage silos set amidst blowing grass, turned right after an apple orchard, and wound down into the state park with 1.7 billion-year-old pink quartzite cliffs overlooking a deep crystal-line lake. Anna had started her climbing here, and the first day that she had gone out with a group of female friends who called themselves the Crag Hags she had been so frightened after the first few climbs that she almost decided never to return. But she had, and had simply kept taking her fear with her each time, placing it in the small chalk bag she carried on her harness, cinching it up tight so that neither the fear nor the chalk blew away on the wind. Each was used, and worked with. Each had its purpose and could aid her up a climb if properly applied.

Done with religious musings, Sal sang along with "Bye, Bye, Miss American Pie" on the radio, which was a little funny given his Spanish inflection so that "drove my Chevy to the levy but the levy was dry" came out more like "dose my sezy to she lezy buzza lezy . . ."

"How do you know this song, Sal? You weren't even growing up here when this came out!"

"I don't know," he answered, making his hand-sail out the window cut through the wind. "I just really like it."

They parked and hefted onto their backs the old canvas bags of ropes and the helmets lashed together with rainbow-colored material called webbing. Webbing, all-purpose in climbing, was made of seat-belt type material. It was the primary material they used for what they called anchors, which they would temporarily set up at the tops of the climbs. Three pieces of webbing would loop around trees at the tops of the climbs, then meet at an apex, at which point a metal clip called a 'beener, short for carabiner, would serve as the connector point between the webbing anchors and the rope strung through. It was a pulley system. In this pulley system was a climber on one end of the rope and a rope-holder, or belayer, at the other end. Anna smiled at some students' notion that the belayer could haul them up the climb, when in fact they had to actually climb the rock, the belayer only taking in the slack to keep the rope tight on the climber.

This was an extremely safe, bomb-proof type of climbing, as climbers said, so long as the rock stayed in one place. It was much safer compared to what she and Sal did, called lead climbing, in which the lead climber took the rope up with him or her and in essence reset the pulley every several feet, with the metal pieces such as the one that had hit Anna in the head in Eldorado. The cut was still healing. In this type of climbing the climber was "on the sharp end" of the rope. The stakes were much higher than they were with the anchors at the top and the pulley system.

Once a student got used to falling into a harness and relying on the pulley system, she could begin to trust the rope and the system. Still, it was not for the faint-hearted, and a person generally had to have a tolerance for being high off the ground. Useful also was a taste for touching and using rock. Working with the students' fears of getting used to the sensation of climbing was one of Anna's greatest loves.

She and Sal headed up through the woods to the talus slope of loose large rocks and ascended to the base of the cliff as the sun played chase between the clouds and the dapple-green trees of the Wisconsin woods.

"Something's different here today, Sal," Anna commented as she sweated her way up the large boulders flung about eons ago when the cliff shook and settled onto its knees at the base of the lake.

They stopped.

"Some new rock's come down. Wow. Look at that," said Sal as he dropped his pack and headed towards a new pile of large broken rock. New rock didn't have lichen on it, and it was usually bright white or fresh orange or pink, its new broken surface exposed and unaffected by millennia of rain and gnawing microbial growth.

"Watch out for loose pieces. Holy smokes. What happened here?" Anna's mouth dropped.

They stood in awe at the new pile of rock scree that obscured the trail higher up. On the wind blew the smell of rock, solid granite, thousands of years old, crushed and tumbled in a deafening moment whether or not anyone was around to hear it. Ancient snakes having come out to warm themselves on the sun-beaten rock would have burrowed deep, coiling tight and deep against the hard cascade that would have silenced birds for acres.

"Maybe it came loose in those tremors we've been having?" said Anna.

"Yeah, but those couldn't have been enough to do this. I don't think."

"I don't know. I wonder if it's stable enough for us to keep going up?"

"Well, it's only on a part of the trail. Let's skirt this part on the old talus and keep going to the base of the cliff. I think it'll be all right if we just avoid this part. Damn. It must have happened during the night, or you'd think some of the people in the park would have mentioned it. We should report it to the ranger when we're done setting up here," Sal concluded.

Loose scree such as this could be deadly. Stepping on a rock at the wrong angle could let loose an avalanche of limb-amputating and head-bashing boulders, so they cautiously went back and hoisted the gear up again, eventually getting to the base of the eighty-foot cliff.

Devil's Lake had some of the best climbing for beginners that Anna and Sal had ever set up and used for lessons, so they began putting up the anchors and ropes for the group they would meet later, still feeling a little edgy because of the loose rock. As they worked, Anna recalled a climbing party in Yosemite, which was a mecca for climbers in North America. The party had been warned against pulling on a loose block of rock but had done so anyway. When they pulled on the block and it came loose, it severed their rope. It was a long way down for the climbers: they had peeled off twenty-two rope lengths up. Anna wondered what it would be like to contemplate hitting the ground from about twenty-five hundred feet up—did you pass out, or were you conscious the entire time the ground got closer? Did you have time to think about the people who would recover your splattered body, or the loved ones you were leaving behind?

Devil's Lake was significantly smaller in scale than Yosemite. Most of the climbs used webbing around trees for anchors, but some of them required the metal protection pieces. Anna always enjoyed this type of set-up because it allowed her to get creative and use her extensive gear rack. From the top of the cliff the lake beckoned, and Anna meant to remember to ask Sal if they had time for a dip before the group arrived.

Sal and Anna shouted to each other that they were finished, then began the descent back to a quick lunch and a rehearsal in their minds of how the day's teaching would go.

Back down in the parking lot, Sal asked, "You ever worked with kids with epilepsy before? Or know anyone who has it?"

"Yeah, I used to work at a summer camp in Maine where there were some kids who wore helmets all the time—not just for climbing. We'd teach them riding lessons. It's kind of spooky because you never know what's going to set them off. What's amazing is that the horses knew to stop in their tracks if a kid had a seizure coming on. But it was a good feeling to see the smiles on the kids' faces and how good they were with the horses."

"Mmm. Well, I'm just even more alert to our safety today, given the population. I've seen people have seizures before, and I'm kind of surprised the coordinators of the program were willing to do this, but if they judge it's okay, well, then, I'll do my end of it. I don't think we could be any better prepared than we are," said Sal.

"Got that right. Beverly was really good in talking out the possible scenarios with me, and just the fact that they have almost a one-to-one staff-to-student ratio for us today is great. Keep in mind most of them aren't having the big seizures; it's more the petit-mal or absence kind, and the staff know those better than we could." Beverly was the program coordinator for most of the activities the group of kids with epilepsy participated in.

They finished their sandwiches and did have time to run down to the lake for a quick dip before the group arrived.

When the kids ranging from eight to fifteen years old had arrived, Sal and Anna got them herded onto the trail with their lunches and sneakers. A couple of them already had helmets because they had seizures so often they needed protection. Most of them, however, were fairly well controlled on medication. The greater danger for the climbing instructors was dealing with kids who were potentially dopey and not able to respond in their belaying jobs as quickly as they should. But they were a cheery bunch, having looked often at the fragile balance of life and determined to go forward. It was unlikely any of them would be scared away by being off the ground climbing on rock.

When they got to the newly fallen section of rock, Anna halted them and told them all they needed to move gingerly off the trail for a little bit, and that the tremors they'd been feeling lately were probably responsible for this latest rock fall.

"I did feel something a few nights ago when I was at home in my living room," commented Beverly.

"So did I!" piped Kyle, a scrawny, grinning boy with big ears. "I thought I was having a seizure! My mom looked over at me like it was catching!" Several of the kids laughed.

"I was in the tub. I thought my dog was having a seizure and making the bathtub and the water shake," said Melilah, a girl with dark, wavy hair, whose Arabesque beauty belied the fact that several times a year she would lose all voluntary muscle control and writhe with angels and demons wrestling for the ground of her spirit.

All of the kids knew the great leveling experience of epilepsy, which was invisible most of the time, until it sprang up like a snake from out of the rocks snatching them unawares. Some of the children had been placed on a high-fat diet proven to help with the neurotransmission in their brains, some of them had worked with biofeedback to identify the emotional triggers of a seizure; all of them took varying degrees of medication. Only three had been seizure-free for any length of time, so that they could gradually begin to forget the wrenching exhaustion of a seizure and the lurking fear of the next one. All saw life as a series of packets of precious jewels made discrete by seizures.

Anna was strangely moved by this affliction that was the height of metaphor for loss of control. None of the kids who regularly had seizures could ever pursue the lead climbing she did without risk of death, far more so than she faced. Not that she thought everyone should climb; it was just that it was a freedom she couldn't imagine going without. But then, she supposed there were advantages to what they dealt with of which she was unaware, such as that they might feel closer to God because they were closer to death in a more real sense than she ever really was.

One of the younger girls came up alongside Anna as they ascended the trail.

"I have a dog, his name is Arl, he knows when my head gets fuzzy," she ran together. "You should see him. He loves to climb up rocks like this. He's not scared at all, like some dogs are of going up rocks."

Anna put her hand on the girl's sandy hair, which was pulled back into a pony tail.

"Have you had Arl a long time? He sounds like a good dog."

"He is. And he sleeps with me, too. He's twelve, and I'm eight. So he knows me longer than I know him."

"Do you like climbing rocks as much as Arl does?"

"Well, I think so, but I'm not sure. Do girls do it as much as boys?"

"As a matter of fact, they do. And sometimes they're better at it than boys, because they're more flexible and . . ." she tried to figure out how to explain strength-to-weight ratio to an eight-year-old, but gave up and said, "They're just really strong at it. One of the best climbers in the world is five-foot-two and is a girl," she said referring to Lyn Hill, a legend in the climbing community.

"Well, we'll see if I like it. I'm not scared," the girl said, and Anna smiled as she wandered off to one of the other kids in the group.

They arrived at the top of the trail and went through the routine of teaching the students how to belay, keeping each other safe with the ropes.

One of the local rock-gods, a lanky, pony-tailed climber whose name, Ralph, belied his prowess, slid by the group and tersely nodded at Sal. They knew each other's climbing abilities, and had a mutual respect. Sal explained in a whisper to the kids, "There's a guy who's really good at climbing, and who put up, or created, most of the routes you'll be climbing today." The kids turned in awe as Ralph wound his way down the base trail, gear slung across shoulders as broad as his ego.

"I don't care if the guy climbs flippin' 5.15. He's an ass," Anna muttered under her breath but so that Sal could hear. Climbing was rated in difficulty on a decimal scale, ranging from 5.0 to 5.14 for practical purposes. The 5 referred to fifth-classing, which meant ropes were required for safety in ascent. Ralph was old-boy's-club and had little respect for the Crag-Hags, who mostly kept their climbing recreational, fun, and limited to top-roping instead of leading.

Sal and Anna focused on safety and fun for the group, not caring about technique. As the sun curved forward in the sky, the kids raced through a panoply of emotions with the rock as a mirror: fear, abject terror, giggles and nervousness, pride, delight, triumph. Anna particularly enjoyed seeing each child's personality reflected in the encounter between something so inert and unmoving against the carvable human soul. This was fuel for her work. She enjoyed working with kids more than adults because adults were so convinced they had to garrison in their emotions when they confronted the rock face; kids let it all hang out. It was a precious gift they gave her without even knowing they were giving it.

There had been little emoting in the house in which Anna was raised, so like water in a desert she sought it in other people. Even in her young adult life Anna received more response from the rock she climbed than interactions with her mother. Her father—well, he hadn't been able to be instructive for a very long time. Unlike other people, she didn't turn to the lessons of her early life like other people did.

She supposed she had been crippled in some way because of the arid environment of her upbringing, but she had run so fast and so hard from it to the springs of other's teachings that she was able to forget it most of the time. She loved the children's effusive displays of feeling, and she was a sucker for cheesy romance novels and chick flicks. Tiny children with Down's Syndrome, eyes as skewed as their fluffy baby hair, made her weep in coffee shops. Her first boyfriend had said, "You're too much. You're too intense," and so they had veered from one another; she didn't know what was appropriate in emoting, so she became more reserved. With Jonathan she'd come closer to talking from her heart, but even so she had the inkling that that capacity wasn't fully engaged within her.

Anna was comfortable with these kids with epilepsy, because their perceptions of the world were not so far off from hers, she felt. They sensed it too, and were having a marvelous time. Her involvement with them gave her energy that powered the rest of her life.

One of the more athletic-looking boys, Randy, had begun up a climb that would be a challenge for any beginner. Anna walked along the cliff base, her harness clanking with metal, and began encouraging his foot work as he struggled his way up through the cracks and protuberances on the rock.

Just as he had jammed his fist into a hand-sized crack, a tremor began, jarring Anna from her introspection. The quaking was sizeable this time. It was enough to make the kids shout, and Anna and Sal look over at one another. Sal unfroze first.

"Bring him down! Randy, let go! Sit into your harness!" Sal jumped over to Melilah, who was Randy's belayer. Melilah began crying and completely let her hands off the rope, so Sal leapt behind her, pulled her into his waist, and took over the rope handling as Anna struggled to unleash the girl from her harness that was tied into the ground anchor. The girl began crying harder, sandwiched between the two instructors, one of whom was trying to calm her, the other shouting at the boy up the cliff who wasn't letting go his hold on the rock.

"Randy! Give it up! We need to bring you down!" Sal yelled, then began cursing in Spanish.

"I can't! My hand's stuck!" wailed the boy. "My shoulder hurts . . . I'm hanging off my arm and it won't let go!"

"Okay, listen to me," Sal's voice commanded.

Beverly had gotten all the other children unclipped from their ground anchors and had moved them slightly away from the base of the cliff, so they had a good angle on what was happening with Randy about forty feet off the ground. The tremor grew.

"You need to relax your forearm," instructed Sal. "Listen to me! You can tell your fingers to pick up a pencil when you think about it, right? So tell your forearm to relax. Once you relax your forearm, you'll be able to open your fist and then slide your hand out. Trust me. Get your feet on something. Remember what we taught you about finding a foothold first!"

Randy began whimpering, as tears, snot, and fear commingled on his bright pink face. He scrabbled to find his feet underneath him. The tremor still shivered through the rock, and a few of the children screamed as they heard some rock fall farther down the cliff.

Ralph came running back along the base of the cliff towards them, yelling that they had to move because some of the climbs farther down the trail were shaking rock loose from up top. He took off down the trail back to the parking lot, not bothering to offer help.

"Keep your heads straight on your shoulders! No looking up!" yelled Anna at the group. Stupidly, too many accidents happened with people looking directly up into rock fall, negating the usefulness of the helmets they wore.

"Aaagh!" screeched Randy, as the rope seemed to suddenly let loose and shift its angle oddly, from the top. Randy dangled, hanging on his shoulder joint, again struggling to find a new foothold.

"Sal, I think one of the anchors at the top let go," Anna said.

Suddenly, Randy's forearm and hand relaxed, and he fell back from the rock, his feet peeling free, as the harness and the rope took his weight.

"Good boy!" shouted Sal, who began lowering him. Melilah sat down as Anna freed her finally from the anchor, and Sal took over the belay completely, planting his feet firmly in the duff. Melilah was crying a little, so Anna put her arms around the girl's shoulders.

"Let's get out of here!" Anna said, focusing again on the group. "Leave everything. We'll get it later." As if exiting a burning movie theater, the children dutifully began filing down the rocky-stepped path, while the tremor continued, shifting shape and intensity. Trees on the trail seemed to quiver at their roots and their crowns danced. The group made it to the parking lot untouched, to find the van but no other cars in the lot besides Sal and Anna's.

Finally, all the shaking stopped, and they all sat down on the asphalt. Fortunately, no one had been triggered into a seizure with the panic, and for this Anna and Sal and Beverly were grateful. The kids bubbled with the thrill, Randy showing off his gouged hand and inflamed forearm, hero for the day.

"We need to go find out what the hell just happened there," said Sal, pulling Anna aside to confer with her quietly.

"We'll have to find out if it's safe to go back up and take everything down. And find out what happened to that anchor on Randy's climb," Anna worried. "This won't look good to the Israelis, or anyone else, for that matter, if it comes out in the news."

"We did everything by the book, Anna. It'll be all right. But we definitely need to review this and get in touch with the rangers, and the police, too. This kind of seismic activity is crazy. The whole cliff might have shifted. Or come down, like Mt. St. Helen's."

"No sign of Ralph. Told you he's a jerk," she spit out, needing to relieve some tension.

"Never mind him. Let's hope no one in the park got hurt." To Beverly Sal turned and said, "Are you okay to let it go for today? Get them home," indicating the kids, "and we'll talk later? I mean, all in all, I think it was a successful day," he smiled wanly.

Still wide-eyed, Beverly was polite and thankful, but hurried the children into the van and promised they'd talk by phone. She reassured Sal and Anna nothing was their fault, but they still drove away with concern for a lawsuit or at least a letter of complaint.

Anna and Sal planned to come back the next day once the rock fall had had a chance to settle out so they could retrieve the ropes and gear and look at the damage. Anna went home to the shower, anxious to tell Jonathan of the day's events, wondering if the mishap would jeopardize her reputation and the trip to Israel.

10

Jerusalem, the month of Nisan, 35 C.E.

A VIEL SLUNG THE LEATHER bag over her shoulder, checked that her small writing pouch was also around her neck, and went to request some money from her Aunt Miriam for the market at the Royal Stoa of the Temple.

The trip from Capernaum to Jerusalem had been wondrous for her, giving her a sense of open country and freedom to move about that she had longed for in her bones without knowing how deep the urge was. Since she had come to Jerusalem, Aviel had tucked into the routine and relationship dynamics of her mother's sister Miriam and her husband Mordechai. Jerusalem was exciting, stimulating, and she felt well cared-for and protected by her uncle's sphere of influence within the city. She wrapped her head in a blue linen cloth, bid her aunt farewell, and stepped out into the early sweltering spring afternoon.

As she walked past the stone houses of the wealthy towards the Temple, Aviel reflected on how comfortable she had become here so quickly. When she had arrived she had been given a spacious room off the corner of the cool limestone house perched on a small hill in the upper city. The house's servants had made her feel welcome, and gradually she had begun to explore the city.

At twenty-five hundred feet above sea level Jerusalem looked down from a height of land on the Judean desert; within the gated walls of the small metropolis there were two primary hills around which the city centered and was expanding. The affluent and priestly Jewish families lived on the upper western hillside. Across from them was the ambitious Temple Mount built during the rule of King Herod, which had expanded on the already existing ancient Temple. Construction was ongoing even after Herod's death, workers laboring to insert massive blocks of limestone of differing hardness into huge carved-out wooden wheels that would then be rolled by oxen to the next area of scaffolding. On a few days Aviel had sat hidden at a distance and watched such work going on, writing and drawing in her notebook, shyly glancing at the dark glistening skin of the workers as they sweated and heaved the materials erected to testify to Herod's greatness both while he lived and after he died.

Herod's architectural efforts dwarfed anything else in Judea, captivated approaching visitors and pilgrims, and dizzied those looking down from the Temple area onto the streets below. The entrances into the Temple Mount area itself were dark, ornate, and constricting but then led into a sun-soaked plaza in the center.

Yet the center was not really the center: only the High Priest of the Jews could go to the heart of the Temple, the Holy of Holies, on the Day of Atonement for sins, which came once a year. Respectful Gentiles could get only so close to this portion of the Temple. Israelites could come in a little closer; women had a special area within this broader area; and then the Court of the Priests was the next closest access to the sacred center. Aviel's uncle could go into this area, and Aviel often secretly resented that she was unable to join him.

Below the two heights of the upper city and the Temple Mount were the lower city, where the poorer Jews lived, as well as the ancient City of David just below the modern Temple Mount. East of the Temple Mount and outside the city walls was the steep Mount of Olives, from which one could get a spectacular view of the layout of the land. Aviel had lolled under the tiered slopes of olive and fig trees, listening to the rustling leaves in the breeze after she'd had a hot climb up the hillside, passing on the way caverns sinuous with tombs. On most afternoons the limestone native to the area radiated a roseate-gold glow peculiar to the city, like nothing she had ever seen before. Pilgrims coming from far and strange foreign lands to worship at the Temple were not disappointed when they arrived and beheld the central historical monument to their faith, ethereal in the setting sun.

While Jerusalem was not naturally abundant with water in the city proper, its only spring, Gihon, had been supplemented with several pools that had been carved into bedrock to create reservoirs. These served the water needs of the city's population, the pilgrims who needed to bathe away the dust of their travels, and the faithful, who needed to cleanse their souls from the impurities Jewish life continually tried to erase before the One God. Even if Roman paganism could not be imported in this crowning city of the Jews, Herod had nonetheless adopted the Roman aqueduct system to pipe in water from springs from up to fifteen miles away. Some of the wealthier families had cisterns dug under their houses, and Miriam and Mordechai enjoyed one of these. There was even a sewage system within the city, which Aviel marveled at for its sophistication.

The room Aviel occupied had been intended for Miriam and Mordechai's first child, but the boy had died as an infant. There had been no more children. After the crouching pall of grief had finally dried up and blown away from the house, over time Miriam had become fussy and irritable, dissatisfied generally. When Aviel had written asking to come live with them, the motherless woman seemed refreshed to have her niece arrive and was content to give Aviel the empty room, indicating warmly that she should settle herself in.

And so the girl from Capernaum with the reputation had arrived. She draped around the room some colorful swatches of different fabrics she had bought at the market, fabric spun from worms and imported from the east, and lightweight linen the likes of which she had never felt, all dyed in arresting, deep hues that reached their threads into her heart. At the foot of her bed she kept a wooden inlaid chest, and the pallet she slept on smelled of lavender. Miriam had also tucked sachets of lavender in the corners of the room in hopes of stimulating Aviel's cycle; she had heard the stories, and though she had not yet spoken directly with Aviel about it, she felt she would someday because they both knew the pain of being childless.

The house Mordechai had built was a marvel of modern split-level professional construction and occupied about twenty rooms on the hillside. Mosaics decorated the floors, and it had a central courtyard, open to the air, luxuriant with palm trees and succulent plants. One of Aviel's tasks was to water the plants every few days by dipping into the holding waters of the cistern. The house had three *mikva'ot*, the ritual baths all the prosperous families had in their homes—one for the servants, one for Miriam and any visiting females, and one for Mordechai and male visitors. The *mikva'ot* were cut into the bedrock of the hillside and were lined with gray plaster. Aviel would also refresh these with rain water set aside specifically to make sure the ritual bath fulfilled the requirement of being "living water," water that came from a fresh source, for only this would satisfy the Jewish purity requirements.

In addition to the *mikva'ot*, Mordechai had had built a steam bath, in which he indulged periodically and which he would share with visitors. Public bathhouses might have worked for pagans, but Jews were more modest because of the circumcision that distinguished them, and because their modesty reflected the idea that the body and its functions were to be sanctified for God.

Further decorations in the expansive house included frescoes of pomegranates and apples that covered the interior walls of the house; Miriam and Mordechai were not as fond of the geometric designs popular in some houses. But unlike the Roman pagans from whom they borrowed their internal decorating designs, no Jewish household would abide any pictures, whether human or beast, in keeping with the requirements of scripture to make no graven images.

Beyond the house's many rooms were clay-tiled awnings that extended from the outer walls for shaded areas. It was much more space than Miriam and Mordechai really needed, so they were glad to have at least one boarder in Aviel. For its outer raiment the house wore brilliant bougainvillea bathed by the air of the city, which was overall dry but touched daily by the rising curtains of salt air from the Dead Sea several miles away, and periodically by rain.

Mordechai was a religious official like Jairus, but more important because the Temple was the true center of Jewish observance. He belonged to a high-priestly family, was a Sadducee, and was a member of the Sanhedrin. He had a playful side, but in his middle years now, he was simply stolid in his work and learning. Aviel thought he tended to the compulsive side, more so than her father, but she also assumed this was necessary for dispensing the Law as he did.

Mordechai had been trained as a scribe, and he would work with the scrolls Aviel only dreamed about crafting. She had had a hundred questions for him about the practice of being a scribe. While the Law nowhere forbade a woman from being a Torah scribe, tradition permitted only men to work with the scrolls. Over the last couple of hundred years scribes had been concerned with correcting and preserving the Book of the Law, and so there was an increasing emphasis on precision with the written word. Had she been allowed, Aviel would have given her life for the meticulous task.

While Mordechai appreciated Aviel's interest in writing, he could only encourage her in business transactions and her fanciful writings. Jews did not take dictation, but would only copy scrolls and sometimes the less common book form, a codex. Thus, while women were not infrequently used for scribal work in other cultures, the uses for Jewish women were more limited.

Mordechai did concede that his niece's script was particularly delicate, so he encouraged her continued work with Aramaic, Hebrew, and Greek. She wrote rapidly and had developed a system distinctive to her own writing that used a series of slashes, dots, and curly-cues that allowed her to shorten her script and record words even faster. This was particularly useful when she used words repeated often, such as in business or in holy matters. Mordechai thought this quite clever of her and that the trick could find broader business application; but the sacred script used by scribes for centuries was set as it was and so Aviel's ideas would make no inroads there.

Despite their childless state, Mordechai was proud that his wife was well-learned, in addition to her other virtues. A considerable portion of Miriam and Mordechai's wealth had come from Miriam's dowry. She had no siblings, so her father, an ivory trader, had been extraordinarily generous when his only daughter had been well-placed in marriage with a learned man, and Mordechai remembered to express his gratitude. But thirteen years' Miriam's senior, Mordechai had begun having aches and pains in the mornings when he awoke, and on occasion he felt anxiety about the fact that he was getting older and had no children to leave behind as his legacy. His wife dealt with their age difference as best she could, but at some level she did not comprehend his fears and sense of loss that seemed to accompany growing older. While their lovemaking had declined somewhat in recent years, still it was vigorous, and when she was through her period of impurity she steadfastly sought out her husband. She loved to place his hands on her hips and feel the life energy in them; she believed they had something special in them because he spent so much of his time with holy words.

They were a handsome couple, Miriam tall, with bold and dark eyebrows, Mordechai with a strong broad back and unusually straight teeth. It was easy to see they were drawn to each other physically; the fact that they did not have children was puzzling to their families, but the other women in the family had never directly asked after the first death.

Miriam's and Aviel's eyes were similar, though the resemblance stopped there because Miriam was much sturdier-framed than Aviel. If Miriam had any concern about another young woman sharing her household with her husband, she did not show it. For his part, Mordechai cared

about Aviel, but did not find her attractive; his wife was much more gen-
teel in her femininity, and he was by nature monogamous. Along with the
number of servants in the household, the new mix worked well.

Jerusalem was freeing at the same time that it was safe for Aviel. She
no longer felt examined and closed in upon as she had felt in Capernaum,
after the miracle. Here, no one knew her, and her aunt and uncle had been
scrupulous to keep her business to themselves. Still, she did not bleed,
though she felt well overall. But when it came time for Miriam to go to the
monthly *mikvah* bath to purify herself, Aviel did not accompany her.

Talk of Yeshua surrounded Mordechai at the Temple, yet Mordechai
was able to separate off in his mind what had happened to his niece from
the clatter he overheard about the small-town self-made prophet who
seemed reticent to have his name spread. He was aware of some of the
elders' unrest on account of Yeshua, but they could be just like women
in a family gnawing on the smallest of details to create a drama within
tight circles. So he largely dismissed the *lashon hara*, the corrosive gossip,
which was the liquid poison drunk by a majority of people who behaved
as if it were water. At times it was tricky staying out of it all, and Mordechai
thought that some of the people with whom he spent his day viewed him
as superior or arrogant. But he could neither control nor prevent their
judgment. He could simply be at peace, which he maintained well.

This peace he brought home to Miriam. Aviel witnessed her uncle's
conduct while admiring and learning from it. Occasionally she wrote letters to her parents, and missed them, but the person she missed the most
was her sister Devorah. She longed to see her sibling getting older, and
wondered how well she was taking up the household chores. Envy for
the attention her sister now received exclusively from her mother crept
up on Aviel now and again, an attention she had not enjoyed since before
Devorah was born. In her letters Aviel would describe the golden glow
of the city and the sounds and smells of the market, hoping to entice her
sister to come for a visit when she was a little older.

On her way out to the market at the Royal Stoa this bright and hot
day, Aviel saw her uncle coming towards the cool house, back from the
Temple midday for his meal.

"It's hot out there, Aviel. The sun will burn today."

"You look worried, Uncle. Is everything all right?"

"There is talk that Yeshua is coming for Passover this spring, to arrive
soon," he said. "We've had many letters from the scribes in Capernaum, as

well as other cities up in Galilee, about what he's teaching."

Aviel's heart stirred when she heard this, because it probably meant his disciples would be with him, and in the group would be the man John. She didn't understand fully the implications of what Yeshua was teaching that so disturbed the priests in Jerusalem, so she focused on the cheerful content of Mordechai's information.

"Perhaps we could make preparation for them—I mean, for him, and have him eat with us?" Her suggestion was forward; it should really have come from her aunt, but it had come out of her mouth and could not be retracted.

Mordechai raised an eyebrow at her.

"I'll discuss it with the mistress of the household." He paused, then said, "Your idea is a gracious one."

She lowered her head, nodded, and departed from him for the market.

The market was a bustle and flurry of sounds and smells in the Royal Stoa, which was a series of vast columns set into the southern wall of the Temple Mount that supported the largest roofed building in all Judea. While Aviel had never traveled except for her passage between Capernaum and Jerusalem, she was told this hive of commercial activity resembled pagan markets around the world. Here, in less than a year, as a scribe she would be able to notarize financial transactions. Sacrificial sheep and doves were sold here, along with pet birds and linens and pottery and oil and trinkets. One could also change money here to pay the Temple tax, which was half a shekel a person—a high enough price.

The sounds of the market clattered and rang in Aviel's ears, men clamored with buyers for a little more money, a little more, rubbed their fingers together, and declared their sacrifice at such low prices. Today she went looking for garlic bulbs and figs, and as she passed the tight stalls and benches seemingly alive of themselves and hawking wares, she ran her fingers across the colorful tapestries and silken clothing from distant lands. She would have come home with much more than she had been sent for, had she been permitted. Today she only looked, paid her money, and took home her items tucked into the leather satchel. Mayreet, Miriam's chief helper, would know how best to prepare the food.

That evening, after Mordechai had come home from afternoon services and as the sun died behind the upper city, the kitchen help cleared the perimeter wooden benches in the smaller dining area. Before wine, olives, bread, a fish and pistachio dish, cucumbers, dates, and figs, Miriam and Mordechai and Aviel reclined for their evening meal. When they had finished eating and then said the blessings afterwards, Aviel excused herself to write to keep with her nightly discipline. She took a small lamp with her through darkened corridors to an outdoor area that overlooked the city in the dark, under the stars.

As they rested after the meal, Mordechai told Miriam, "Yeshua is coming for this Passover, making the trip from Capernaum. I heard Nicodemus speaking of it," referring to one of the elders who was respected for his learning, and who lived just a few houses down from the couple. Mordechai had always appreciated Nicodemus' sense of humor when it came to discussions they had of their aging versus their youth, and while Nicodemus was a Pharisee and Mordechai was a Sadducee, they shared a mutual respect.

"Are the elders worried? Do they have a plot yet for how to deal with this troubler of men?" Miriam asked tongue-in-cheek.

Mordechai's mouth turned up on one side. "There's just a lot of buzz, no honey anywhere nearby, as far as I can tell. He's in this wave of prophecy that's been going around, not precisely a Sadducee or a Pharisee, and certainly not an Essene," referring to the elite group of Jews seeking strict observance and purity who cordoned themselves off in the desert near the Dead Sea.

Mordechai continued, looking tentatively at his wife. "I'm not sure where he plans to stay, and I wondered if you would consider opening our house to him and perhaps a few of his followers. Not all of them, of course—although we could, I suppose; we have enough room—I'm sure some of them will stay with relatives or friends. Unless they all decide to sleep up on the Mount of Olives, being from the country. Maybe they'd be more comfortable there than enjoying the city's luxuries!"

Aviel had come from the small portico in which she had been writing, intending to go relieve herself, just in time to hear her aunt begin discussing a visit from guests.

"Well," Miriam chose her words carefully, "I would be happy to have Yeshua and perhaps his closest men, but I think the others—including any women who follow him—should stay elsewhere. We don't want to overburden Ehud and Mayreet and the other servants," she said, referring to the cooks, the bakers, the gardener, and their children.

Aviel ducked down behind the half-wall as she headed to the bathroom. Her heart pounded and she felt silly, an eavesdropping servant-girl. Her eyes widened as she heard her uncle discuss the particulars of Yeshua's visit.

"If I understand correctly, his closest companions are a threesome—some fishermen named John and James, and then a man named Peter, all from the Galilee area. Would that number be acceptable to you, my dearest? Four?" At this he reached over to her luxuriant hair and stroked it.

She tilted her head, pressing his hand into her shoulder with her cheek.

"That would be quite acceptable. That many I think we can accommodate. Will you send word? Do you think they'll accept?"

"Well, again, my understanding is that they have never refused anyone's hospitality, including hosts the elders consider—well, less than savory. So I think we'd probably be tolerable."

Aviel swallowed. John would come stay with them. She would have to see Yeshua face to face again. She had escaped Capernaum, but it seemed she could not avoid those two. Would her perception have changed any since the last time she had seen them? Lingering in the thought, she crept on her knees along the wall to its end, then stood and padded back to her room. The realization dawning on her, she sat down in a heap on her bed. Was she bound to this set of men, the one so unearthly but who had brought her back to life, the other very much in the physical world? She smiled at the thought of John's hair and eyes, then pulled her attention back to her hand, turning it over and back again. Not since that day in Capernaum had her hand stopped burning; she had learned to live with it. Writing softened the ache, but then if she wrote for hours the hand would cramp up, so she had to let it rest. Miriam and Mordechai were unaware of the pressing need in her writing hand. Perhaps she would ask Yeshua about it.

Uncurling her legs from underneath her, she went to the clay basin, dipped in her hands, then splashed her face. The cool water cleansed and rinsed away the day's heat. Unlike some of the other young women her age, her face was clear and untroubled. Sometimes she would have traded her barren status for a pitted, young fertile face full of pus, just so she could be known to have entered the ranks of women. About that she could not ask Yeshua—maybe he had cursed her in some way—but she certainly had held such a conversation with him in her head more than once.

That night Aviel dreamt of the catacombs potholing the hillside on the Mount of Olives, with a salt fog that breathed in and out of them and scrolled around like Hebrew script.

11

Preparations for Passover swallowed the household. Because Mordechai was so closely related to the Temple, his family's precision with adhering to the provisions in the Law was obsessive—or so thought Aviel. Even with her father being a religious ruler in Capernaum, the Passovers she knew were more light-hearted, more feeling than thinking. Still, her mother and her aunt both became so exhausted with ritual details that Aviel cringed at dealing with them both.

An entire new set of bowls came out, thin and shallow, and painted red, brown, and black. These were separate from the ones used the rest of the year, and far more delicate than the ones Aviel knew in Galilee. Storage shelves for the common dishes were cordoned off with rope so that those dishes would not be used by mistake, in a sanctifying gesture of purity.

In the back rooms for preparation, Mayreet told the story to the other help of how one year Miriam had all but blatantly accused that year's guests of stashing one of the special bowls in their robes at the end of the night as they were leaving, because not all of the dishes had been accounted for when the table was cleaned. In the end, the bowl was found when it was discovered one of the young girl servants had miscounted, but it was too late to preserve Miriam's shellacked reputation as a hostess.

Under a Jew's roof there was an entire ritual getting rid of all leavening, in remembrance of the night of Exodus when their ancestors had had to flee Egypt at the last hour, having no time to wait for the bread to rise before they departed. In the ten days before the celebration, the house was emptied of all leavening for bread-making, and whatever was found would be either sold to a non-Jew or taken out the southwest gate of the city and burned in the trash heaps of the valley of Hinom.

Hinom, or outer Gehenna, was a valley turned into garbage pit and was bounded by some imposing cliffs that abutted the city's southern wall. The poorest of the city came to scour whatever detritus had been cast into the valley, so whenever the slaves went to get rid of household refuse, they always went in pairs, for safety. Aviel had been there once, and she had been overwhelmed by both its stench and barrenness. She knew that pilgrims often approached the city from this plain below the imposing rock walls, but she could not imagine anyone perceiving Jerusalem as a shining beacon of faith when this was their first view of the city.

Aviel thought the Passover preparation excessive. Nonetheless, she performed the tasks asked of her. In the meticulous period before the holiday, Miriam threw a daily snit over some small item, concerned that the house would not be presentable enough for its esteemed guests. At least, Aviel thought they were esteemed, but she wasn't entirely sure; certainly their political agenda seemed different from her uncle's, and from what she understood, they had aroused tempers in a number of towns throughout Judea.

The men who were coming to visit were not Essenes, the secretive group that would exit the city gate near the walls of Hinom and move to caves near the Dead Sea, keeping their knowledge and their strict observances of the Law to themselves; nor were they part of either the Sadducee or Pharisee groups, who ruled over ritual observance as they nipped at each other constantly like rat-haired underfed dogs. The contested turf was the Law, and each felt they had the correct interpretation that would ensure the survival of God's people in the face of Hellenistic and Roman influence. Had she been her uncle, Aviel thought, she would have quickly tired of the squabbles and power plays. She was curious to see how Yeshua and his followers sidestepped the pomposities, even while they gained strength in the face of the existing powers, both Jewish and Roman.

Yeshua was expected to arrive within the next couple of days, and when Mordechai had told the elders of his intentions to host the prophet for Passover the men had become quiet. Some of them had gathered in the sunny portico of the Stoa at the noon meal.

"What does he intend, coming to Jerusalem? Why doesn't he celebrate with his family, up in Galilee? Is he like the pilgrims, coming in awe, or does he come with a political agenda against Rome?" asked Nicodemus, speaking what many of them thought. It was a reasonable question; the balance between mollifying Rome while maintaining Jewish observance and upholding Jewish interests was a tension that Nicodemus felt his people could not long withstand.

"His learned teachings for us are welcome, at this point, but we want him to answer to some of what we've heard about what he's doing, some of the more, eh, unusual . . ." Nicodemus didn't want to get into specifics about the healings they'd heard of. No one had yet asked Mordechai about Aviel's experience, though Mordechai was certain they had talked about it behind his back.

"All good questions," responded Mordechai. "But he will observe Passover just like the rest of us, and we intend to show him hospitality. I'm sure he'll be a gracious guest, as my wife and I will be gracious hosts. He may be from the upcountry in Galilee, but he's a Jew. Regardless of his leanings and interpretations. It could be rather interesting, actually."

At this the elders were again quiet.

Mordechai left them in their fine robes to mutter amongst themselves. He preferred the quiet of the warm, dry day for the opportunity to finish his work in solitude, until he had to hear some cases of financial complaint later in the afternoon.

That evening, after the daily prayers were complete, Mordechai crossed down through the valley and felt the twilight pressing deeper as he walked home. A stray cat slunk through the covered market stalls, following him as if he had something to offer in the way of food. Some days he grew so tired of the politics, he wished he could have been an itinerant teacher of Torah from the country, just for the peace of it. Yet he knew Yeshua's ministry was turning out to be anything but peaceful. Curiosity about the rabbi's plans had gotten the better of him in issuing the Passover invitation, so in some ways he was just as guilty of gossip as the rest—but he thought it purer, somehow, if he spoke to the source.

Maybe it was the hustle of Passover Mordechai despised, though he knew he was not involved in the worst of it, that being left to Miriam and now Aviel. In the alleyways his sandals scuffed the dust as he mused about the questions he intended to ask the man from the north. Did he ally with the Pharisees more than the Sadducees? Or with any sect? Why did he continually challenge Sabbath laws? Did he intend to confront Rome? If so, where could that possibly lead? What was his vision? What was he calling himself? And what really had happened with Aviel? If his mind had been a flame it would have lit his path in the dark with his wonderings.

Jairus's letter accompanying Aviel had been sparse; the subject was indelicate. Mordechai had pried Miriam for details, but at first she had kept Aviel's lack of monthly flow to herself. He could tell something wasn't right, though, and finally asked, when the young woman had not gone to the *mikvah* with his wife and when she was slack about not wearing her head covering when she went out.

Questions. Sometimes it seemed as though his life were nothing but questions, the majority of which were never answered but were quashed by the massive granite burial stone that was life, constantly rolling forward.

He trudged up the hill, tired, but glad for the walk this evening. He entered the foyer and kicked off his sandals, sat on the bench, and poured water from the jug over his caked feet. Mayreet, in blue linen, appeared from out of the twilight and presented him a soft cloth and a smile, then retreated.

God forbid he should bring any unrest upon his household because of the impending visit! It began to sink in for Mordechai that he might have gotten himself into something he ought not. At least the visitors weren't expected until tomorrow, and while he imagined he would spend the evening soothing his wife's anxieties about final preparations, he planned to savor the quiet until they arrived. The greatest miracle Yeshua could perform here, Mordechai thought, was to create serenity in the household while he was here. Maybe he could ask him for that.

"Good evening, Aviel," Mordechai said as he came into the dimming light in the center courtyard fragrant with blossoms and palm greens. A songbird balancing in a delicate cage trilled its greeting.

"Uncle! How was your day?"

"Well! Today I got into a discussion with a young man on the preparation of the scapegoat for the Day of Atonement."

"Tell me about it! I am grateful that all of our sins get placed on that goat and the goat is put out from the community to atone for us, but I have always wondered where the goat goes, and what becomes of the goat!" She smiled at him.

He chuckled. "You are a strange young woman, Aviel. You would have enjoyed speaking with this young man. I can't say as I've had anyone wonder about the well-being of the scapegoat before. That goat is treated like royalty before it is sent away. It is groomed daily, bathed in scented water, and fed the best grain." Mordechai paused and looked at her to see if she was following him still.

"But really, Uncle, what becomes of the scapegoat when it is sent into the vast wilderness? Does it die of starvation? Are its eyes plucked out by vultures and it wanders until it is set upon by jackals and eaten, so that our sins are thus destroyed?

"Aviel, you understand the story of the scapegoat is a metaphor, surely?"

"Of course! Of course. But it captures my imagination—really, what happens to the actual goat you use for the sacrifice of sins? Does it survive and find goats from other years past and mate with them, thus metaphorically multiplying our sins? Maybe this is why there is so much evil in the world! Because the sins have not actually died, but have proliferated."

Mordechai just looked at her with a raised eyebrow. "You're writing too much, I think. You need a husband and children."

"Well, a husband wouldn't keep me from my fanciful thoughts, and I would only tell my stories to my children. Along with their instruction in Torah, of course," she added.

"So keep dreaming, my niece. If you had to deal with the nonsense I have to each day, your dreams would be driven out from you—like the goat. Ahh," he groaned, and his hands came up to rub his face. "Whether it's a man protesting that his neighbor absconded with his sheep and sent them into Hinom after dark, then the man broke his toe retrieving them and wants restitution, or it's my superiors wrangling over the Temple tax, there are days I can only throw up my hands." He sighed. "But enough of complaining. How was your Pesach preparation today? Was anyone too unbearably cranky?"

"Actually, preparations were fine today. Just finishing up some final touches. I think we are well-prepared; everything seems . . . under control. Your wife is in better humor than she has been," Aviel grinned.

"What are you writing now?"

"A letter to my sister, Devorah. I do miss her—seeing her grow. She'll be so much older, taller, now. I wish . . ."

"Would you like her to come visit?"

"Yes! Oh, yes, I would dearly like that. Is it possible? Would that be all right with you both? I'd show her the market, and the trails up the Mount of Olives, and . . ." Her words rushed out, and, laughing, Mordechai raised a hand to stop the onrush.

"Of course! We would simply arrange a chaperone for her. Perhaps Mayreet and some of the others could go fetch her. They'd probably welcome the trip. Let's talk about it further after Passover."

Just then they were interrupted by a loud pounding on the wooden front doors. Aviel jumped up and looked at her uncle, frozen. He called for Ehud, Mayreet's husband, who came in jogging in and went to answer the knock. Aviel began backing out of the courtyard towards a passageway in shadow, where she could just see who was requesting entrance while she remained hidden.

Ehud swung open the heavy entrance and there stood three men, covered in dust and sweat, dressed in simple clothing.

"Yeshua bar Joseph, James, John. We have arrived earlier than we expected . . . will your master forgive us and house us for the night?" Yeshua touched his fingers to the mezuzah on the doorframe then put his fingers to his lips. The others reached around him and followed suit.

Ehud bowed his head, invited them into the foyer and offered them oil to dab on their foreheads, then turned to find Mordechai.

Mordechai tucked his chin to his chest, and when his head rose, he had veiled his dismay at his guests' early arrival; he started forward towards them with his most welcoming face. He would soothe Miriam later.

"Good evening! What a delight to have you arrive early. You must have made excellent time. Come in, come in, wash your feet. My wife will be delighted to know you are here. Yet—I thought you were four? "

"John has a house here, and he has offered it to Peter, who has some business to attend to. It will be more convenient for him that way. Peter also has been invited to Passover by old friends of the family. I hope this does not put you or your wife out?"

"Not at all, not at all. We are grateful you can be here. Ehud, see to a meal, and prepare these men's sleeping quarters," directed Mordechai.

Aviel poked her head out from behind a colonnade and took in the men.

Yeshua was as she remembered him, but even dirtier. As he bent down to rinse his feet, his hair dangled forward, stringy and pushed back from his forehead, full of travel grime. John stood behind him, half a foot taller, his hands larger than Yeshua's, his nose stronger and his jaw sharper. James, incidental in Aviel's observation, merely served to fill up the foyer. Regardless of who they were and what they were doing with their learned and earnest engagements, and perhaps because she had been through death and back, she could only see them as men. Her interest lay in the connecting threads between the words of their mouths and the meditations of their hearts. For the next few days, at least, this criterion would be the measure by which she scrutinized them. Any significance they had in the outside world faded into the shadows along with her.

Yet she was unsettled to see them arrive so soon. From another passage she heard her aunt's approach, saw her robes billowing out behind her, and Aviel decided to go to her room quietly. Aviel caught Mayreet's arm as she came by and explained to her that she had eaten earlier, was tired, and content to go to bed early. She wasn't sure how she would sleep for the night, knowing John and Yeshua were in the house, so she decided to focus back on her letter to Devorah and keep scarce for the next two days before Passover.

12

AVIEL WOKE, GROGGY. A late morning sun penetrated the window hole in her wall and burned a brilliant square on the floor. Rolling over to the bedside bench, she pulled to her the scribal table Yohanon had made. With her fingers she traced the carved olive leaves, smelling the air of Galilee in her memory and seeing Yohanon's facial creases. It was her habit to take out her stylus first thing in the morning, writing her dreams or the first muzzy thoughts that came to her. She didn't know anyone else who did this, and when she had tried explaining it to Miriam and Mordechai, they looked at her blankly, as if she had somehow sucked all the words from them. So she kept the practice to herself, but found it the most freeing time of her day. It always improved her mood.

This morning she wrote secretly, behind closed doors, of her observations of John and Yeshua. Nothing was hidden in this description of her life to herself, and she would have done anything to keep it private. Word images for Yeshua eluded her, but John she rendered in minute feature. If this scribbling had any practical use she doubted it, but her stylus dipped into the ink repeatedly. Writing was a flight, a freedom, in a world that protected well-to-do women like birds with clipped wings. While she could have chosen either Aramaic or Greek for her language, she settled on the most sinuous—Hebrew—because she liked its appearance and its ancient history for her people.

She wondered if the men visiting the house were aware of her presence, if they knew she had come to live here with her aunt and uncle. If they didn't, they would be surprised at the evening meal. It was too far past the morning meal, she could tell by the sun in the sky, for her to greet them; they would have been long gone for prayer and study at the Temple. This cloudless day would scorch the city streets and the olive groves on the heights alike. She laid the stylus aside and rolled off her pallet to groom herself and dress.

The house was quiet, so Aviel sought out Miriam. She imagined that Miriam had been none too pleased that the guests had arrived early, and if she couldn't find her aunt, she would seek out one of the servants to get an accounting of how her uncle had handled any temper tantrums.

She was not disappointed.

"She's gone to the market," said Mayreet, referring to her mistress "Oh, she was gracious at table when we pulled out extra fish and olives and bread for those men, but she let your uncle have it later. Not that I can hear anything through these walls and doors—they're so thick," the woman excused herself.

Mayreet had come from one of the poorest families in the lower city and counted herself fortunate to be so well-employed. She would do anything to keep her position and was keenly aware that gossip did not sit well with her master. Better than anyone, she knew her mistress's kindnesses as well as her rare but considerable excesses of mood, and she usually worked with the swings better than did even Mordechai. Between the pendulum of Miriam's depression and her giddiness, Mayreet walked a thin, steadying line of influence in the household; Ehud backed her up. Now, with Aviel's new feminine presence in the household, the servant woman was doubly alert to the fine equilibrium of emotions.

True, Passover was always a difficult time—it brought out the excessive in almost every woman hosting the holiday, Mayreet had observed over the years. This year was particularly challenging, with the new men in the house, so the servant had encouraged the mistress to leave the house for the morning on the pretense that they needed more nuts for the *haroset*, the nut and apple mix that would symbolize the mortar used by the Hebrews for bricklaying when they were slaves in Egypt, before Adonai had freed them. Miriam had gone willingly, seeking diversion

Aviel thought she would seek out her aunt, so grabbing a bag and covering her head she told Mayreet over her shoulder that she would be back shortly. It was after the prayer time, so she hoped to catch both her aunt and perhaps a glimpse of their visitors. She would be sheltered by the anonymity of a pilgrim-crowded market.

When she arrived, the Stoa was in chaos. Women wailed, dogs barked and chased fluttering birds, men's voices were hoarse from screaming. At whom, Aviel could not tell. Children scrabbled for coins scattered on the ground as she took in the hectic scene. Crushed grapes and figs oozed underfoot and goat cheese smeared on the ground made the stones so slippery that people's feet gave out from underneath them as they hurried to escape the melee. She was in time to see Yeshua at the far end of the market grasping a booth, throwing it on its side, and clearing out its occupants with what appeared to be a braided whip of reeds. Aviel stood, stunned, next to a colonnade, surrounded by swirls of people while scanning for her aunt. What was he doing? Where had he gotten the whip?

She spotted Miriam crying and cowering in the center of the plaza, horrified at her guest's indignity. Aviel picked up her skirts and ran to her, startling her out of her misery as she grabbed her forearm.

"Come, we have to leave! Come with me!"

Miriam, eyes and nose running, nodded in recognition. They made their way back across the valley, climbed the hill faster than they ever had, and ducked back into the house. As Mayreet came to them she could clearly see that her mistress and Aviel were upset, so she took their head coverings from them and ushered them into the central atrium, then sat them on a bench near the small pool.

"Sit! Sit! My word, what's happened? Sit here. I'll bring you some tea," and she disappeared into the kitchen area.

Miriam sobbed. Aviel rubbed her hand on her aunt's back. Awareness of her aunt's volatility with emotions had begun to dawn on her with the Passover preparation, so she realized she should just keep quiet until the crying stopped. Sometimes, she had observed in puzzlement, people were afraid to cry—as if they thought they would never stop; but in reality, any two-year-old taught otherwise. The crying inevitably stopped at some point. So she believed crying was good for a soul, even if initially it was shocking to a person's façade.

Mayreet returned with tea leaves and honey in hot water, and Miriam began sipping.

Finally, she said, "How can I have that man in my house?" But the thought dead-ended.

Some of the servant's youngest children had crept up behind some columns to see what the ruckus was about, only to be shooed away by Mayreet.

"We saw Yeshua in the market," Aviel explained in answer to Mayreet's raised eyebrows. "He destroyed it. He threw the tables of the moneychangers about, and the doves, and the produce . . . it was a mess. I have no idea what he was doing!"

Miriam spoke again, filling in the scene. "It was after services. He came striding up the steps—he must have planned it because the whip looked deliberately made, not hastily—and he came running up with his robes flying about him and began yelling at all the people, turning over their tables. He was livid, and he screamed at them, 'You have made my Father's house a hiding place for robbers!' He slashed and tore and . . .' her hands waved and she could not finish because her tears began again.

Aviel and Mayreet sat quietly, not sure what to say.

"Mordechai said Yeshua might be coming with an agenda, but this is crazy. The man must be crazy." After a few more sips of tea, Miriam had begun to recover, and heat built in her words. "How shall I have this lout under my roof for a sacred meal? How do I know he won't shame us, tossing over our own table, the table we have so thoughtfully set for him? I can't have that!"

At that point Aviel and Mayreet looked up as they heard Mordechai slam the front door. He paused for a moment before he strode into the center of the atrium, then he took in the scene with his wife and niece and servant.

"Were you there?" His words were clipped, terse.

Miriam looked up at him and began to cry again, and Aviel said, "Yes, she was. I came at the end of it."

Mordechai paced. The songbird held quiet in its cage; only the small pool trickled. The women watched him, pensive.

"Well," he said taking a breath and turning to them. "We'll still perform our duties as hosts. You women will recline with us and eat, as he requested, rather than serve us. I don't know when he plans to return here, but we will welcome him and entertain him as he initially requested, do you understand me?" His voice was firm, wooden.

Miriam looked aghast at her husband. Sitting at table with that man would be like sitting with family while there was a large gray Persian elephant in the middle of the table that everyone ignored. No amount of beaded coverings or baubles could cover such a monstrosity. How would they look beyond it sufficiently to conduct a civil conversation? With family, the ties that oozed back years into each person's childhood had to be tolerated, but why did Miriam have to put up with someone she didn't know and for whom she had certainly lost respect?

"We'll make it work. I will make it work. Trust me, my love," he said as he came over to run his hand over Miriam's hair and kiss her. He smiled as best he could into her eyes, then exited the house.

Miriam looked at Aviel. Feeling dull, the older woman declared she was suddenly tired and needed to rest. They ate a little lunch, then went to their individual rooms to nap, recover, and be refreshed for the Passover meal in the evening.

13

YESHUA HAD RETURNED TO his hosts' house with James and John, but Peter was still absent, having excused himself the day before to the house of some in-laws. John and James had taken a steam bath to relax from the morning's uproar, but Yeshua was nowhere to be found within.

Later in the day, Mordechai came home from the Temple. After a few brief words, the men all retired to their rooms to put on fresh robes, then gathered in the larger dining area where the servants had placed colorful embroidered pillows on the benches and floor so the participants could recline during the meal.

Miriam and Mordechai entered in their finest garb for the occasion. The fabric was uniform so that wool and linen were not mixed, according to the Law. The night that was different from all other nights began, with Mordechai leading the ceremony, repeating the narrative they all knew so well from childhood—the drama of their ancestors' escape from Egypt wrought by the mighty hand of God.

The ritual was lengthy, and by the time the first food was consumed at about eight-thirty in the evening, Aviel was famished. The story of the Jews' freedom from Egyptian slavery unfolded. As Mordechai recounted the ten plagues, the listeners dipped their fingers into their wine glasses and dotted linen napkins to represent each plague that had leaked the life blood out of the Egyptians, who, despite being the Israelites' captors, were nonetheless acknowledged as children of God. Because of this fact the Israelites' cups of wine (and therefore joy) were less than full. Just as God hushed the angels from singing when the Egyptians were swallowed up by the Red Sea, so, too, were Jews not to celebrate with a full glass of wine at the destruction of their conquerors.

Ehud's young son had hidden a piece of unleavened bread, which later in the night the adults would ransom with a colorful bird or wooden toy. The drama lived and breathed from generations past, bringing into the room with it a body-memory of a people, along with its yearnings for the future. Aviel loved the yearly ritual, and her heart cried for her family this night, but her relatives' version of the ancient rite was an exhilarating rendition.

Whatever words Mordechai had exchanged in the afternoon with Yeshua and James and John had made it possible for them all to sit together, but Miriam had not had the opportunity to speak with her husband at any length before the meal got underway. Aviel and Mayreet felt Miriam's palpable discomfort radiating about her.

Likewise, Aviel had a heightened awareness of the guests at her table. Her observation was two-pronged: first, she felt the love between Yeshua and John was a net that would catch and pull in all others. Clearly, the youthful John was Yeshua's favorite. John and Yeshua's hearts beat the same rhythm, they laughed at the same things, their eyes quickened over the same small cares of their daily experiences. What they lacked in relationship with their own families they had made up for in friendship with one another.

Beyond that, Aviel felt John's response to her. Because she sat nearly opposite John, she hoped the unseen cords running between them were blanketed by the ritual and would go unnoticed by the rest of the table as its participants paid attention to the formal procedure that evening.

John reclined on finely wrought cushions and leaned up against a bench. Aviel noticed the length of his toes in his sandals, even the line of his legs under his robes. He had cleaned his hair and face and beard and applied a light coating of cedar-scented oil to them. Under eyes hooded by dark lashes he glanced over at her now and then and smiled. Rapidly she would turn her eyes away, then stealthily looked back at him as he laughed and talked with James, who was a much smaller and slighter man with bad teeth. They were animated, jostling each other, obviously familiar with one another since youth.

As they listened to the ancient story of freedom, they staved off their hunger before the full meal by snacking on unleavened bread and a dip of horseradish, vinegar, and honey. Mayreet's method of preparation involved cutting the horseradish and letting it sit for several minutes before adding the vinegar, which gave it an extra bite. She loved seeing people's faces pucker as they felt the hot burning sensation spread behind their ears and bring tears to their eyes before they sucked in cooling air.

A milder dip of cut-up apricots and raisins and nuts was passed around the table, along with cut garlic soaking in olive oil. Almonds toasted with honey and salt from the Dead Sea were mixed with raisins and set out in small earthenware vessels. For another dip there was humus made of mashed chick peas, olive oil, red wine vinegar, mustard, garlic, oregano, red onions, and fragrant fennel.

Finally, the story took a rest and their stomachs welcomed the main meal of braised leeks and onions, a salad of olives and endive, and early, cool cucumbers sliced lengthwise with the skin scored in a spiral pattern. Miriam passed pomegranate seeds, a symbol of fertility, to Aviel, and the young woman blushed the color of the wine in her cup.

Leg of lamb that had marinated for two days in pomegranate juice, garlic, mustard, and rosemary was the highlight of the evening; this was then finished off with the sweet, pulpy, aromatic flesh of ananas melons and the bright pink-orange flesh of Persian melons, and finally a bitter, strong drink made of chicory.

When John was not occupied with food or with James, it was as if his and Aviel's skin would touch across the table's divide, their very body temperatures matching. It was as if they engaged in a dance separate and apart from the other bodies at the table, the earthbound bodies arid, while Aviel and John flowed along in torrents of underground caverns beneath all that was said during the course of the evening. The strain of keeping her face muscles placid and engaged at a superficial level, while her soul was being carried away on the current of John, eroded Aviel's endurance as the night wore on, exhausting her reserves, but it was sweet torture she would endure threefold if she had been asked to again. She felt sure he felt the same; certainly, he felt something—it could not simply be happening all in her own head.

Yeshua interrupted, rousing her from absorption once again.

"We need scribes in our gathering. Most of our number do not write, or read. In our movement women are engaged the same as men; the Kingdom of God is not exclusive to men," the Galilean guest smiled. Suddenly the conversation was focused on Aviel, she realized, and she had to pull herself up out of the flood into which she had been swept. Simple, Yeshua's sentences hung in the air. No embellishment could have pinned Aviel's attention more. Clearly the table was waiting for a response from the young woman, or, barring her, at least her uncle, speaking for her.

"I hope to receive my commission next year," she managed, swallowing a bit of rosemary-rubbed lamb and looking wide-eyed at Yeshua. "Since, as a woman, I am not permitted to copy scripture or take dictation, I would like to make copies of books made to order for private parties and booksellers. Though it would make sense for me to write the *mezzuzot* and the *tefillin* because my handwriting is so small," she added, referring to the tiny copies of the Law Jews put in their prayer phylacteries and on their doorposts, reminding them to inscribe God on every aspect of their hearts and lives.

Yeshua nodded in approval. He let his suggestion go, but asked Aviel. "Do you write beautifully, then?"

"Well, I would not be the first to say so, sir, but I do love what I do. It's as if my hands—that is, my hand—has something in it. I use shortened forms of words, sometimes, that others wouldn't understand. But it allows me to write more quickly. Of course, this practice I use only for my own purposes. And I am very private with what I write for myself. The words from our hearts should be guarded so, don't you think?" she asked boldly, putting down her napkin, unafraid to raise her eyes to his. Bathing comfortably in the purifying waters of his gaze, it was as if she could meet his heart in her eyes, perhaps because she had been to death and back; she knew he had the same courage as did she about death, while other people lacked this and could not look directly at her when she chose to delve into those recesses. John was the only other person with whom she felt she could engage this way.

"To the contrary; I believe we need to speak our hearts. But this will put us at odds with those in power," and here he glanced at Mordechai. "Sometime you'll have to show me this shortened form of communication," he concluded graciously, looking back at Aviel. He turned his attention to his host and, indirectly, his hostess. "You've taken a risk, having me here tonight." Because Yeshua had already spoken with the Mordechai and his friends before dinner, this was offered for Miriam's sake.

"Somewhat, yes," Mordechai said, flushing slightly. "My elders were not happy about the idea, though they didn't directly say as much. You know that we're descended from aristocracy, and the preservation of tradition is crucial to us." He paused. "But clearly, you aren't afraid to speak truth to power." Mordechai bored into Yeshua's face.

"And you are a brave man for offering me sanctuary, although I come to pluck the string of untenable tension between the imperialism of Rome and Jewish observance. Such as my actions indicate today," Yeshua added, referring to the debacle at the Temple earlier in the day.

He chewed some lamb slowly, then continued, pressing his point and already knowing the answer. "What would the Sadducees say about this woman, raised from the dead?" he indicated Aviel, who bowed her head, uncomfortable at being the topic of conversation again. If she could have covered herself with pillows or slunk out of the room she would have. Suddenly her toes became very interesting.

"We would dispute that she was dead, rabbi." Mordechai did not flinch from the challenge. "Just as you feel free to contradict the elders' wisdom, so must I contradict you, despite your learning. And heritage. There is no resurrection of the body, rabbi; you know we believe this. One's legacy is through one's children," he added with thin sadness, thinking of his own infertile legacy.

Aviel felt as if she had been placed in the middle of the floor for examination, once again the object of commentary, although those commenting were unaware of their effect on her.

"Is there not resurrection?" the young prophet asked. It was rhetorical. When Yeshua spoke again it was almost to himself. His hands were on his thighs, both palms up, relaxed. "You argue with the Pharisees for temporal power, over the details of the Law, but you neglect the life of the spirit in the process. Adonai knows this. Your sects will be destroyed, along with the Temple."

The unctuous elephant had raised its head with the prophecy, and the table fell silent. No one could see around the beast.

Quietly, Aviel said, "I was dead, uncle. Now I live. I have no fear of death now. I wished for it, even. It was peaceful there." The elephant heaved itself off the table and dragged itself out of the room into the shadows beyond.

The young woman folded her hands in her lap and again lowered her head, feeling the constant burning of her hand like a live and foreign creature in her flesh. At the same time, Yeshua's presence pulled on her attention. When she had tried to explain to people in her life what had happened to her, her words had been sharp-edged stones skipping across a stilled pond. When she spoke in Yeshua's presence, the edges of the stones caught the water and sank. He was the bottom of the pond, holding her meaning. When he was present, she was unconcerned with the ripples of other people at the surface.

Miriam sat in shock, at a loss as hostess for how to make the dinner proceed smoothly, pleasantly. Blinking, she asked, "Do you like the sweet baked garlic?" but her guests could only look at her, not comprehending. "I learned it from a woman from Damascus. The lamb, also."

Relief came when Mayreet and Ehud rustled in and began clearing the wooden platters from which they had all eaten the meal. The interruption provided some breathing room and James cleared his throat.

John looked over at Aviel and smiled at her, reassuring her with his eyes. He was used to this type of direct confrontation from Yeshua. Conversation again shifted to lighter subjects, and at the end of the meal they began intoning the blessings after meals, somewhat more heartily than usual, to close out the evening of celebration.

Aviel went to her room that night and wrote copiously. She wrote of her longings for home, the smells of the lake at Capernaum, the simplicity of her parents' house, Yohanon's laughter, her mother's peculiar love, the donkey, and especially Devorah. She wrote of her ache for John in phrases she didn't know she commanded, her yearning for a man whose longing for connection could go as far as hers and from whom she did not have to shield her gaze in a gauze of superficial politeness, as she found she must do with all others, because they could not tolerate the concentrated depths of her own look. She sat, hand cramped, under a dim lamp until her eyes were bleary, and it wasn't until the stillest hour of the night that she finally put down her stylus and rolled onto her pallet.

With a single birdcall fanning open the dawn, Aviel awoke. Sliding out of bed, she pulled her robe about her, tied up her hair with a cloth, and padded into the atrium. On the far side of the small pool sat John, tracing a finger in the marble basin. Aviel stopped on the cool tile floor, feeling the small mosaic pieces under her toes. She watched him for a few moments, then glided towards him.

He caught the movement out of the corner of his eye and saw the woman who had filled his dreams. Rising, he faced her. She paused, eyes riveted on his face, until he moved so close to her that they were within one another's space and she could smell his skin and feel the breath of his life flowing softly from him. He reached for her hand. Its familiar tingling ceased, and her hand warmed as if she were holding a golden orb. He interlaced his fingers with hers, raising her arm, playing the fan of her hand, running his fingers across every one of hers. She sighed and closed her eyes.

A cool morning breeze rustled through the atrium as the sky began to change from gray to early cerulean. Feeling the luxuriance of the moving air against his skin, John pulled Aviel closer and placed his lips against the line of her forehead and hair. The linen of their robes touching now, an invisible field drew them into one. They stood this way for several minutes, breathing the same cadence. Finally he spoke.

"My days are focused on Yeshua and his ministry. But you fill my night mind," he confessed. He absorbed her lavender scent, kissed the top of her head, then pulled her into his body.

"Come with me, come with us," John pleaded. "You will see what Yeshua is working . . ." But even as he spoke, his words trailed off and he became confused; his divided loyalties pushed to the forefront of his mind. Confounded, he felt the human pull of his body, while at the same time he knew Yeshua called him to a spiritual journey. He pulled back from the embrace, but his hands were still interlaced with hers, his eyes searching hers. He had grown uncertain of himself despite this closeness he had so long dreamed of, as if he had recklessly fathered a love that he could not in fact support.

At a deep level John knew he possessed an impetuosity that Yeshua had pointed out to him. But in his youth he was unable yet to own this side of his nature, so he turned his uncertainty into a challenge to Aviel. He questioned her spiritual commitment, believing rightly that she was not sufficiently swayed by Yeshua's ministry so far. His tone was more interrogating than he realized.

"You have seen the works he can do. You live and breathe it. You must believe he is the Messiah . . . you'd have to believe that to adhere to our group, to come with us . . . Do you believe he's the Messiah?" Unwittingly, their love hung on the thread of her answer.

Despite this different orientation John had suddenly taken towards her, Aviel could only wonder if his body was pulsing like hers. Surely his words were coming from another realm, underwater, like her thoughts.

Reeling herself in, she swallowed and collected herself. "He may be the Messiah. I don't know. But I also know that he is a man, because I sat at table with him, and I watched him clean his feet when he came in that door. He probably snores at night, too. And yet I know he's unlike any other human being I've ever known. I have touched his flesh. He has touched mine. Have you touched him? Do you hug him, or wash his feet, ever? Because I know this connection with him. He dragged my very soul from outer darkness back into the living light. I trust my own experience, but I'm young. I haven't had enough experiences with men to know whether or not they're trustworthy," she said, remembering Nathan, and looking at John as her eyes narrowed.

"I don't know precisely what makes Yeshua so different from the other prophets going about prophesying, like the one who was baptizing, but I know that what he did with me was extraordinary. He may have the power to gather people to him, and to pull back the dead from Gehenna. He'll need support in his efforts with Rome and with the Temple authorities. No one who challenges the priesthood the way he has can continue on his journey without help. Perhaps he has help beyond what we see. It's not an accident that he's chosen you, John. But you're young too—you're barely older than I am.

"Maybe you're right that we can't mold a romance between us like a piece of pottery while at the same time you focus on Yeshua's purposes. But I can tell you that as of now I am unwilling to be an object of his mission. I left Capernaum to escape scrutiny, so I could live the life he brought me back for. I don't think I'd have that if I went with you. And I am too irreverent, after all," she added sadly.

"I have to focus . . . I have to focus . . . but," and here John capitulated, "I also believe the natural love between a man and woman could only fortify my commitment to Yeshua and to God." He took her shoulders in his hands. "I feel this with every breath I take, every dream I have of you. I've given up everything for him on this journey. He knows it. I don't believe he would deprive me of my heart's desire."

She was slow to respond as she listened. "Am I your heart's desire? Or is Yeshua? If I came with you, would you soon drop everything to follow after me the way you dropped everything to follow him? What do you suppose Yeshua would think of that?" She doubted him now.

He looked up at her, disbelieving the way they had wrestled their way around the issue.

The quietness of the dawn began to broaden into sound as one of the servants began moving about down one of the halls, so Aviel and John stepped farther apart. John rose but took Aviel's hand. She looked back down the hall towards her room, then turned back to him.

"Do you know your letters?"

"Yes, but I'm not a learned man . . ."

"Good. Never mind how sophisticated or simple they are. Write me. Send your dreams, what you learn from Yeshua, from your own heart, and in time . . ."

His eyes pooled, pleading with her, and she tried to pull her hand from his. He drew her in closer again, kissed her with the hot fierceness of a young man, then released her and turned to go to his room.

Aviel watched his departure, her eyes reservoirs. Then she, too, turned and went to her room. Slowly she let down her hair and climbed back onto her pallet, touching her fingers to her lips for the lingering warmth of his kiss. She lay for a long time listening to the birds rising in song before she drifted back to sleep.

By the time she awakened later in the morning, Yeshua and John and James had left for Galilee. It would be nearly another year and cycle of celebrations before she saw John again.

14

Madison, fall 2008

THE TRIP TO ISRAEL had gone forward. There were obstacles to overcome at first, because the Ein Gedi school had wanted an inquiry
done on the incident at Devil's Lake. But once they had seen the seis-
mographic readout from the tremor and looked at several photographs,
a committee had come to the conclusion that it was an act of God. This
term was a puzzling one to Anna, one she couldn't quite wrap her head
around, but in and of itself that was ironic, she thought, given the history
of the nation which she would be visiting.

So the young instructor was on track for leaving in a week, and she
had gotten in order her passport and traveler's checks, small amounts of
toothpaste and face cream in a plastic see-through bag to show she had
no intention of blowing up the plane, her Hebrew-to-English dictionary,
and the website printouts on the climbing site. Over the summer she'd
taken a beginning Hebrew class at a local synagogue, but then found out
that the Hebrew she learned was for reading Hebrew in the prayer book
whereas the Hebrew she would encounter in Israel would have only con-
sonants, no vowels. Still, she figured it was better than nothing, and she
had enjoyed learning the new alphabet, which reminded her of Tolkien's
runes of Middle Earth.

The rock fall at Devil's Lake had been cleaned up by a local conserva-
tion group and the Crag Hags, and a new footpath had been created out
of the shift. Several of the routes were different now, with all but one still
sound for climbing, so all summer Anna and Sal had taken groups up to
the Lake—nervously, at first, until they trusted the rock again.

At the same time, she had continued teaching riding lessons at the
Bush Brook Stables and helping out with its chores. It was easier for her
to put aside the climbing part of her life than it was the riding part when
she went away on an extended trip, and she felt sad to leave behind her
efforts there. On a sparkling clear September day she headed for the barn,
the scent of apples and hay-fed horse dung on her pants and shoes. As she

left her apartment, she stuffed some carrots in her pockets and petted the
cat as she exited. She'd had a long weekend to herself since Jonathan had
been away at a conference, and she had enjoyed the respite.

On the drive through the dimming fields of summer, bright red-
orange Indian paintbrush relieving the burnished fields, Anna contemplated Good As Gold, the horse she had been working with lately. He was
a short little model, bright-eyed, decked in a wheat coat and platinum
blonde mane, tail, and eyelashes, a Palomino—a sonorous name suiting
the beauty of his coloration. A freeze mark on the left side of his neck,
under his mane, indicated he had indeed come from Wild West country,
captured under the big sky out of canyons, then was tagged and tracked by
the federal government's Bureau of Land Management, which catalogued
the existing mustang herd. Atrociously grown-out, curled-up hooves
made him look knock-kneed, but because he was so averse to touch, the
blacksmith would need to sedate him to trim his feet, and the farm just
didn't have the money yet to pay the massive sum for putting a horse
under anesthesia.

Anna frequently turned her attention to the most wounded, hurting
mustangs that Moira, the gray-haired and arthritic owner of Ever After
Mustang Rescue, had rescued. Often, the horses would be prematurely
placed with owners whose hearts were in the right place but who had no
knowledge of how to deal with wild horses. Sometimes the horses had
physical injuries, but more commonly they were simply terrified of being in captivity and could not be trained as could domesticated horses.
People would buy the mustangs for, say, a teenage daughter, thinking they
were fulfilling her romantic dreams, only to find out that they had a horse
that could not be trained or ridden and was even dangerous as it tried to
adjust to the enclosed living space of a stall.

Having acquired Gold at a sale in New Hampshire, Moira trusted
her gentle training style could rehabilitate him after his previous owners
had deemed him incapable of being ridden. If he could not be mended,
he would have a safe haven at Bush Brook for as long as Moira could keep
the persistently poor farm propped up and running. But Gold held more
promise, Moira believed.

With Moira's agreement, Anna had taken this particular horse under
her care, knowing, too, that at some level Gold had something to offer.
But on this morning, Anna ended up in the wrong place.

Moira was on her own mucking out, working in the first and third stalls, which sandwiched Gold's. Anna was mildly put out by this, knowing Moira's movement, slight as it was, was inclined to keep the horse from settling into that quiet sanctum they had so recently found with each other as she had begun being able to lay a hand on his shoulder, and even brush him on a few occasions. When he had first arrived, she had spent an hour just trying to get within his space, and he backed away like a bar of soap that seemed to have other places to be.

"The horses are a little skitzy this morning," Moira tried chatting, taking into account all thirty occupants of the stalls on the dilapidated farm. When she got no answer, she asked Anna about her upcoming trip. Anna's travels always mildly put out Moira, and, like Jonathan, she was none too happy to have her help leave. Still Anna responded little, trying to discourage conversation. She had put in way too much time with this puzzlingly wounded horse and disliked having to interrupt the progress they'd been making to simply socialize this mustang so he could be purchased by someone able to handle his upkeep and training. She had wanted to get him to a point of being able to be consistently groomed before she left, because in her absence he would almost certainly forget some of the progress they had made.

Gold was reticent on a morning that wafted smells through the barn and distracted all the horses, causing them to prick their ears. Anna stood near the front of the stall, but Gold was pressed up against the back wall, paralleling the stall door, lipping up loose strands of hay from his floor.

Feeling emboldened by recent small progress they had made, Anna moved gradually into Gold's space, enticing him with carrots. Today she wanted to brush him. She was aware that she was pushing into his zone, but she sensed he was tolerating it. He stopped eating and watched her. He didn't threaten to spin, didn't back away at all, which had been his modus operandi; he just wasn't letting Anna clip his halter with a rope.

She pressed on forward toward his head. Coming closer to the back of the stall, she fished for the metal D-ring of the halter under his jawbone, listening to him blowing out his nostrils, which indicated relaxation. He ducked his head again just as she leaned toward his head with the clip, so she stepped back, growing frustrated, but intent on keeping her humor. Again she reached.

With a firecracker bang against the wall he jumped and spun, and instantly Anna was in the back corner where his hind end had been; he was now facing the front of the stall, quivering, and she was cut off from escape out the stall door.

Anna's heart flapped in her chest; her limbic survival brain sharpened. She knew this was the exact wrong place to be. Being in the back corner of a stall with a startled horse, the horse's butt pointed at her, was not conducive to her coming out of the stall unbloodied or unbashed. She felt her fear rising from her gut to her throat, the sweating, honest fear, the fear that was designed into the human-as-animal. The fear-for-a-good-reason, the I-could-get-the-bejeezus-kicked-out-of-me fear. No psychological fear of failing, or confronting one's boss. It was fear inspired by two tons of hooves lined up and ready to aim at Anna's cranium, poised for her next wrong move.

Gold shivered under his skin, also trapped and frozen by their positions, waiting on Anna's action.

Then a whisper shift made all the difference inside the stall that had become Anna's shrunken, immediate world: she became aware of her fear. She noticed her body and where it was in space, in a way she had never been aware of during a climb. Her heart and sweat and breath tapped out information to her. In that instant Anna made her choice to step outside and above the fear, choosing not to identify with it, claim it, even though she couldn't physically step anywhere other than where she was. Palpably, the charged atmosphere in the dark corner dissipated with her change in focus.

It was the same choice that had defused potential falls, as well as arguments with Jonathan. Consciously, Anna chose peace over fear; immediately the decision tipped the balance in her favor. She stood quietly alongside the wall, keeping her eye on Gold, soothing the tightening in her throat just enough to speak to Moira who, like a guardian angel, was still mucking out in the adjacent stall.

"Um, Moira, I think I need your help, but . . . I'm not sure how," Anna leveled her voice. Moira rested her manure cleaning fork up against the stall wall and came to stand outside Gold's stall.

"Okay, I'll open the door," she began in a quiet, calm undertone, "and you get as close as you can to the wall." It wasn't the first time Moira had seen danger of crushing, staving in of head, or death by trampling like this with a horse frightened and uncertain.

Anna had taken command of her fear now despite the predicament, making every conscious effort to set her position out of her mind as she concentrated on sidling along the wall quietly, gently, making herself small, out of the range of Gold's hind quarters, and around to the front near his head. Gently, left foot in front of right, hand on the wall for balance, shoulders hunched, eyes on him. She dove for the stall door and wanted to call out "safe!"

Once outside safely, Anna chewed over with Moira what had happened.

"Are you okay?" Moira asked as Anna took her position at Gold's head at the front of the stall again. With her up front now in her proper place he backed a few steps toward the corner. He breathed normally now and seemed calm, the quivering gone.

"Yes, fine, just a little shaken, though," she said.

"Well, these things happen, and it's a good lesson usually, because you know you won't do that again."

Anna appreciated the assumption.

Later that night, she sat on the couch with Jonathan and told him of the incident; she needed to unload the impact of the episode, though it had been more mental than physical. Maisley lay quietly on the carpet in front of the sliding glass doors, licking her paws.

"There are no accidents, you know . . . I just wonder how this fits in." She was agitated, trying to find meaning in the fear-evoking event.

"And I'm worried about you flying half a world away? Have you ever considered working with normal people, and normal animals, maybe?" Jonathan said, exasperated.

"Yes. No thanks. I think I'd die of boredom. Why is it so difficult for people—for you—to understand that working with the horses and the people I do is like mining jewels from the earth? I can't think of work I'd rather do. It's about trust, you know? Getting those horses to trust me, enticing young climbers to trust one another as they learn the systems—it's precious work. It makes them go to a deep place where they have to pull on reserves of what makes them tick. I get to have my finger on the vein of every emotion coursing through the body of a creature who's struggling with elemental fears and basic faith, confidence, even dependence on human beings. They're metaphors for me. I'm not doing anything different from what a special ed teacher does in the classroom. Or Tina, working with autistic kids," Anna said, referring to Jonathan' twenty-six-year-old niece. "My work has integrity, and that matters to me. A lot."

Jonathan was quiet, just listening as Anna spoke her soul. "It doesn't pay anywhere near as much as you could earn though, and you know it." He got up and looked out the windows at the lake.

Maisley whimpered a little, as if needing to go out to the yard.

"So I'm smart. So I could be a lawyer or could have invented Microsoft. So what. God doesn't care whether or not you're a member of MENSA when you die. God cares about what you did for others, that you created as much good as you could for others, in the end."

"Hmm. Where's all the spiritual inspiration talk coming from all of a sudden? That idea of creating like God does, albeit on a smaller scale, is Jewish, by the way. Just in case you didn't know. But in any case, it sounds a little to me like you're just trying to please God, like children try to please their parents or someone important to them."

"I suppose I try to please just as much as anybody else. I think we all do; we want to be liked and accepted. But that's not why I'm thinking about God. You know, it's a little daunting going off to one of the holiest places in the world. It makes me think about this sort of thing. Why has this trip come for me now? Like I said, there are no accidents. I really wonder about this place I'm going to be visiting, why it matters so much to them all so that they've been killing each other for centuries over not just how they see God, but where they see God—the importance of Jerusalem, and the political divisions of the land. "

"I expect you'll get educated and find some surprises when you're there," Jonathan said. "And I think you'll be surprised to discover how 'unholy' most of the secular Israelis are—they're rather cranky, in fact. Probably from living in a militaristic state all the time."

"Why doesn't your Judaism matter to you more?" Anna dropped the question in his lap like an unwanted, muddied object the dog had found in the back yard. Within the question's abruptness Jonathan sensed her pushing him away again, but he bit.

"It matters to me . . . I just, I don't—I don't know."

"What matters to you the most? The culture? The history? The modern State of Israel? God?"

"It matters to me that my people have a five-thousand-year history. But I don't know if I even believe in God."

Anna's heart contracted with a squeezing sensation, and she was silent. She felt an ice wind blow through a divide that had lurked between them, a divide that seemed to be growing. That Jonathan was not religiously committed she had known, and that he harbored deep resentments towards the religion in which he had been raised because of his personal history she could respect, but the basic summation that he was uncertain about his belief in a moving life force, an intelligent design, left her at a loss. She saw too much sweeping connectivity in her daily life to feel detached from a God, or a higher power like alcoholics spoke of, or the Universe espoused by New Age people (although that phrase was problematic because she had assumed that God was even greater than and encompassing of the "universe").

"You think all this is just good luck?" she swept her hands around the warm ochre tones of the room, the dim lamps upon the walls, the view out on the lake, silver tonight and placid. Honking geese flying south for the winter punctuated her question. "How can you breathe, move, live—love, even—without thinking there's something greater than you behind it? How can you have been brought up with Hebrew scripture the way you were and have no belief?" She had wanted to ask him these questions for quite some time. They weren't getting any younger.

Maisley whimpered a little louder and wiggled, but Jonathan and Anna still ignored him.

"Look, the concept I have of God is of an old man with a white beard who sits up there," here he gestured toward the ceiling, "and dispenses lightning bolts and frogs and lice when he's pissed off. Or creates inexplicable suffering for Job and doesn't answer." His tone was heated now. "There are no accidents? Are you serious? How can you even propose that with the horrors of humanity we know about? What kind of a God allows those women in Darfur to have that look in their eyes that you see on TV because they're dealing with the residue of rape? And I'm not the first one to ask how the Holocaust could have happened, or where God was during that. What about all the millennia of destruction human beings have exacted on one another, from mass executions to the tiniest pains in individual lives that are otherwise quite easeful, like ours? Do you seriously think you have potable drinking water because your karma has been cleaner than an Ethiopian orphan's?" He was close to outrage now.

"I can't begin to know the answers to those large questions," Anna glowered at him. They were quiet. Then she added, "But I like the questions. I like that you at least ask them. I don't know about the massive horrors you're talking about. We're so globally connected and aware now, with computers and the Internet. But in our individual lives, I believe there are no accidents. Call me stubborn."

"Stubborn. If you say there are no accidents, you get into the whole thing about blame. If someone gets cancer and you tell that person there are no accidents, that guy will think you're blaming him for creating the cancer," Jonathan argued.

"Why? I know I've heard people say that, but it's ridiculous, making that correlation. It's a non sequitur. Just because something happens doesn't mean you have responsibility, or should take the blame, for it. But it's still not an 'accident.' Maybe you had something to do with the cancer; maybe you didn't. Maybe God had something to do with the cancer. Frankly, I think it's a little . . . narcissistic . . . to conclude that just because something bad happens, and it's not an accident, that it's therefore your fault."

"You're arguing both sides of the question—you can't have it both ways," he interjected.

"Why not? Don't be so black and white. It's a paradox. The view you're protesting against would say that you're all powerful, that you're God. Which you're clearly not. It's just like, if a problem gets solved in your life, maybe you can claim you had some influence, because you can be a creator in your life, have some influence. And maybe you can't. Maybe God solved it for you. Or someone you've never even met. We only take blame and credit, we only think we're completely responsible, because we operate as such individuals in our society. You know, we've lost track in our modern society of the web of connectedness in which we live, and it's true we can't possibly figure out all the strands. But we can sure try to understand more of them. If we claim there are no accidents, we deny and blind ourselves to the possibility that we can have an influence, we can create. What happened today with Gold was not an accident. There are no accidents."

Just then Maisley piddled on the floor.

"Including that one?" said Jonathan, as he jumped up to go get the paper towels and cleaner from the kitchen. He apologized to the dog and let her out to wander.

Once that was cleaned up, Anna and Jonathan sat opposite one another on the bed now, eyeing one another, feeling the partition between them. Anna had gotten off her high horse but was still somewhat riled.

Great, thought Jonathan, this probably means no sex tonight, and she's leaving soon.

"I should go. I'll call you tomorrow," Anna said.

"Well, you don't have to look so morose. Look, I'm grateful you're okay, that the horse didn't batter you to death."

"Yeah, thanks. Me too. I thank God."

He looked at her. Maybe this whole spiritual interest she evidenced was somehow behind what he loved most about her. Or maybe it was what pissed him off the most, because it had no end in sight. Or maybe it was just her hair and the curve of her forearm, her neck, her hips. He was tired, and wanted to zone out to some television if she wasn't going to stay.

"Talk to you tomorrow," and he kissed her goodbye.

That night he slept with a well-relieved dog next to him.

15

Madison to Israel

ANNA'S APARTMENT WAS COZY and comfortable on the crisp cool Tuesday that she packed her bags for the lengthy overseas flight the next day. Flights to Israel never flew on the Sabbath but had to arrive in reasonable time for people to get to wherever they were going for the Sabbath, so the departure and arrival times were a little screwy. The next Sabbath she would spend in Ein Gedi, so she was sorry to be missing the day of rest in Jerusalem, because she had heard from talk in the Hebrew class she was taking at the synagogue that a peace fell over the city when the shops and transportation shut down. Only one day a week off seemed an abomination to her, however, and she wondered why the Israelis weren't stressed out from working six days a week. Maybe they were and that was partly responsible for the continued bloodshed.

While she would be gone ten days, she would be largely occupied with familiarizing herself with the safety practices of the school, their policies and gear, and the credentials of their instructors. After the visit she would create a school-specific guidebook so the instructors could quickly and easily learn the climbs they would use. Between her tight schedule and taking into account the time difference, she'd have little time for tourist activities. Yad Vashem, the Holocaust memorial museum in Jerusalem, was high on her list, and she had some interest in the Western Wall of the old Temple, but the majority of the trip would be work-related.

She hadn't even bothered to pack any climbing gear except her harness, shoes, and chalk bag, not wanting to mess with trying to explain to security what the metal objects were on her climbing rack. There was probably a means for flying with gear now, but she would just use whatever institutional equipment the Ein Gedi school used; this would also give her a sense of how current their safety systems were and if they were safe within the context of the site they wanted her to prepare. She had told them she would need a cordless drill for drilling bolts into the top of the rock, and she doubted that the airlines would like to see her bringing one of those with her. Nir had assured her the school could obtain a Bosch drill, and that she would have use of it.

Kitty would go stay with Jonathan, who was always happy to playfully torture the frightened cat, getting him drunk on catnip and teasing him with a peacock feather as a toy. At Bush Brook, Moira had complained loudly and t'sked about the length of time Anna would be gone, but Anna treated her grumbling as background noise. One of the girls who took lessons had been ecstatic to come in and help with the mucking out—more power to her, thought Anna. What the girl didn't know was that she'd be hooked in no time by the perpetually crabby Moira to keep up the heavy and smelly task.

The entire rock gym was shut down for plumbing renovation during the time Anna would be gone, so Sal had teased her that she wouldn't be missed at all. But he was envious.

"I hear the limestone there is harder than even the *meleke*, the hardest type they have. Excellent surface. I can't believe you've never climbed on limestone before! You'll love it. Get lots of pictures and e-mail them to me from the school, if you can. Climb safe," Sal wished her.

"Yeah, you too," she wished him back, referring to the young Spanish woman he had hanging off his arm. "Crevasses can be deadly. You don't want to fall into any."

He grinned his answer.

On a rainy day, Anna's early flight out of Milwaukee was on schedule, and she bade Jonathan farewell with some regret and trepidation. Anna suspected they were both thinking it was good to have some time apart, but neither openly said as much. The tension in the air was broad and unpleasant, and both looked at the ground and the airport display cases a lot more than each other. Anna hugged him with as much depth as she could, and knew she would miss the smell of his skin.

The flight itself would be long, about sixteen hours all told. Anna had brought her acupressure wrist bands to help with the nausea from turbulence and the smell of diesel fuel she sometimes experienced on flights. She also had the most recent John Grisham novel and some sleeping pills to pass the time.

Her seat was about halfway back in the plane, next to an exit, and she did indeed feel very competent to handle an emergency exit should it be necessary. She just wasn't sure, if she needed to leave the plane prematurely, if she'd be called upon to float in an ocean or speak Polish in the event of a land evacuation.

Next to her sat a large black woman from Baltimore who had introduced herself as Edna when she had struggled into her seat. Her hair, close to her head, was gray at the temples and dusted white irregularly around the rest. Lines made their home on her brow, around her eyes, the corners of her mouth, even near her ears. The vigor in her conversation belied her seventy years.

"How you doin', hon?"

"All right. And you?" Anna was a little more of an introvert than riding on planes generally accommodated, but she began to suspect that on this flight she wouldn't get much else done besides talking with Edna.

"I'm fine. Left Pigtown this morning."

"Pigtown?" Anna blinked. She didn't quite know what to say, but inadvertently glanced at Edna's girth when Edna said the word. She blushed as she realized her unspoken thought, but Edna didn't seem to notice.

"Pigtown's a subdivision of Baltimore and it's called that because the pigs used to be run to market through that section of the city. I'm kind of on the edge of it, 'cause mostly it's white folks live there. My son, he lives in the John Hopkins area, but I bet you didn't know that's one of the most violent parts of the city. There was a doctor shot once coming out of the hospital into the parking garage, going home one night, so I told my son he should move into Pigtown with me. But he doesn't want to. Mmm."

Anna forced a smile.

It turned out Edna was also a narcoleptic. Anna had never met anyone with the condition, so when within seconds of speaking Edna's head dropped and her mouth went slack, and she began to snore, Anna looked over at the person across the aisle, looked back at Edna, then tucked her chin in and looked at the seat in front of her as if it would explain.

"Don't let that bother you," Edna said on awakening a few minutes later. "People around me just get used to it. I don't mean to be rude or anything—I just can't help it. The doctors have done all sorts of sleep studies on me and all that, but no one seems to know what to do. I just live with it, hon."

Anna shrugged and smiled.

"What you reading?" Edna went on. "John Grisham, mmm. I think I read one of his once. Liked it. But I read the Good Book almost all the time, you know. The Bible. It's got the best stories you could ever want in there. You want drama, the Bible's got it all. Miracles, love stories, tragedy. Don't need soap operas, or celebrity stories on the front page of the news. Been reading it most of my life, since I was fifteen, when I got pregnant with my son, Darius, the one who lives near Hopkins. He won't take any interest in it."

And then she was snoring again. Anna considered how hard it must have been for Edna to raise a child if she was falling asleep all the time, so she hoped for Edna's and Darius's sakes that the condition hadn't started until recently. While Edna dozed Anna glanced over at the Bible laid out in Edna's lap. It was leather bound, gold-embossed, with a maroon silk string in the middle of the binding for a page marker. She saw that it was turned to Mark, chapter 5.

Anna began reading and vaguely recognized the story of a woman who had suffered from a constant hemorrhage, sought out Jesus, and boldly touched his garment for healing, when Jesus was on his way to raise from the dead the daughter of a man named Jairus. It struck her as she read that the story was lacking in descriptive detail. She recalled that this had been her experience the few times she'd read the Bible, and she wondered how it managed to entrance so many people given the peculiar dryness of narration, which seemed to conform to the land in which it was set. It wasn't exactly riveting reading, she thought, but Edna must have found it so, for some reason. Just as she finished the story of the girl who came back to life after having died, Edna woke up, and Anna apologized to her seat-partner for reading over her shoulder.

"That's all right, you go on ahead, look over my shoulder. Any way someone can do a little theological exploration is fine with me." Edna looked closely at the strained look of politeness on Anna's face and decided to leave the subject of God alone.

"So, why are you going to Israel?" Anna asked.

"Well, hon, I'm going to see where Jesus was born! It's not such an easy thing to do these days, Bethlehem the way it is with the checkpoints for Palestinians and the wall and all. But I been to the Israel twice before, this'll be my third, and I can't wait! It looks different to me every time. This time I'm going for longer. Ever notice how things look different with time, the more you look at them?" Here she couldn't restrain herself. "The God I knew when I was five is not the God I know now as an adult, so I have to keep looking and asking questions, I figure. I don't know a soul there, but that's where my soul is, I know it. I just couldn't wait to go see where Jesus lived and breathed and walked. And this trip I'm going to stay a whole six months, to see if I can get to know some people and practice my Hebrew. The first two trips I did with my church, but this one's on my own. Renting a house from some friends of a friend."

And again she fell asleep.

Anna thought it must be exhausting to have narcolepsy and hoped the woman at least got some solid sleep at night. She also speculated about what the body was trying to communicate with such a condition. She doubted horses ever had narcolepsy.

Putting on her headphones, Anna hoped Edna would give her some respite when she next woke up. As she tried to relax, eyes closed and listening to some Dvorak on her iPod, she contemplated the passionate religiosity of the people around her in contrast to Jonathan's Judaism. And then there was Edna, who believed so strongly that the Messiah had already come that she tackled her obesity and her narcolepsy to pursue what she so fervently asserted—that Jesus was God. But this was contrary to what the majority of the people on the airplane believed, judging by their black clothing, black hats, and long beards.

Jonathan had warned her about the bendies and bowies, as he sneeringly called them, meaning the orthodox Hasidic Jews who were so particular about praying at the right time during the flight that they were up almost constantly, bobbing and bowing in the aisles as they crossed time zones, their curled side-burns bouncing like miniature slinkies. One of them kept brushing against Anna as she was trying to sleep during the night, so she almost bit his head off, but thought better of it. Perhaps they would arrive safely and on time because of all the effort he was putting in. Anna concluded she was too tired to figure it all out.

About an hour out, when the small bathrooms in the back of the plane had become thoroughly fouled, Edna woke with a snort and looked at Anna for a long moment. She began speaking even though Anna was clearly listening to the headphones.

"What about you? Why are you going to Israel?"

Anna glanced over at Edna, removed her earpieces, and with exhaustion showing on her face said, "Sorry?"

"I'm wondering why you're going to the Holy Land. Most people who go there go out of strong conviction. What's your reason?"

Anna ran her finger around the cup indentation in the tray table in front of her then answered, "I teach rock climbing. There's an outdoor education school near the Dead Sea that wants me to set up a climbing site for them in Jerusalem." She hated to go into the dog-and-pony show, explaining what she did. Edna seemed to sense this, then asked her about her family.

"Well, I have a . . . boyfriend, I guess you'd call him, in Madison," but Anna felt a little strange about telling Edna about the fact that she was in an arrangement other than marriage, thinking the Christian woman might judge her.

"MmHmm. Don't your folks want you to get married? A woman your age? What about kids?"

Anna squirmed a little, and she felt that she could have simply put Edna off on account of asking questions too personal, but for some reason she didn't. Whether or not it had to do with Edna's being a religious person with a weight of moral authority Anna wasn't sure, but there was comfortable depth and maturity to the woman that made Anna feel she could confide in her.

"I would like to have kids, but—well, Jonathan doesn't really want to. I think he's afraid he'd be just like his dad in raising them. And he's Jewish, and I think there's something in him that wants his kids to be raised Jewish, but he doesn't exactly know and won't look at it very deeply. So we've just sort of been in this limbo for about four years now," she finished lamely.

"Pardon my saying so, but it doesn't sound like there's a lot of conviction there. Passion. And I don't mean in a physical sense, of course. If I found myself in a relationship like that, I'd be asking why."

Anna, miserable in her cramped seat, could only look at her the tray table, which had not grown any more interesting.

"Oh, I'm sorry, maybe I've said too much. Getting older and this narcolepsy thing tends to make my tongue loose. There's not a lot of time for mincing words. What about your folks?"

"What about them?" Here Anna became guarded. Simply because she was honest didn't mean she had to divulge her thoughts and feelings. This woman, whom she had only just met, was already poking into her soul enough as it was.

"Well, I mean, are they still alive? What's your family like? Got any brothers or sisters?"

Relenting, Anna thought, What could be the harm? The woman was asking, let her know. So as if she could leave the information behind her streaming back into the ether with the jet trail, Anna told Edna her family history in brief.

"My mother and father were high school sweethearts. They were both really smart. My mom probably had an anxiety disorder, no way to know for sure. My father was an Army chaplain and was killed in Viet Nam. My mom kind of lost it after that, and would go into fits of rage sometimes—when I think back on it, all I can think of was maybe it was when she was going through menopause. She never married again. I'm an only child. She lives in a small town in central Wisconsin, where her family is from. I've got lots of cousins, though, some of whom I'm in good contact with."

Edna took it all in, and Anna could tell by the softness in Edna's face that the woman had set judgment aside as she listened. It was a gift Anna had seldom experienced, and she was grateful. They were comfortably quiet for a while after that, then both women fell off to sleep.

They were roused suddenly when applause broke out the moment the plane touched down in *eretz* Israel, the sacred and spiritual homeland for the Jews on board, as well as the Christians. Somewhat more rested and thinking clearly, Anna felt relieved not just to get out of her seat, but to also leave behind the personal discussion, no matter how safe Edna had turned out to be. Anna's neatly packaged explanation of her family's history returned to its place, and the young woman looked forward, as had become her habit, to a new adventure.

Going through customs at Ben Gurion airport, Anna was pleased to discover the process less arduous than she had suspected, although young army guards stood watch with automatic weapons, reminding her where she was.

She thanked Edna for the conversation, wished her well, and they exchanged cell phone numbers.

"Just in case," Edna said. "You don't know your way around here, and if you get in a jam, you just call me. I know a thing or two about this place. I even know a fair bit of Hebrew."

Anna thanked her and thought ironically to herself that she did, indeed, intend to get into a jam—a crack on a rock face, specifically.

Ein Gedi had arranged a driver for her, and, fortunately, his English was very good. He chattered away as Anna passed out asleep in the back seat, barely noticing the landscape flying by, while they drove a circuitous but politically safe route towards the Dead Sea.

16

Israel

ANNA WOKE IN THE back seat of the cab and felt Jonathan cradling her face in his hands, only to discover that it was really the naugahyde seat covering. Wiping the drool off her face, she asked the driver how far they were from the school, and he laughed at her when he saw the creases and polka dots impressed on her face.

"Soon, soon," he said.

Desert dust whipped by, but what Anna noticed most when she rolled down her window was the air: waves of salt thread hung in the air, like beads from a psychedelic 1960s doorway curtain. The threads thinned, shimmering and coating the air and Anna's hair and skin and tongue as the cab descended below sea level. She sank into the ancient land of patriarchs and matriarchs, a land ossified in layers of memories of civilizations and anguishes.

Ein Gedi itself was an oasis in the desert, palm trees and figs and willows suddenly gracing the surrounding dryness as they rolled to a stop on the hot tar in front of a utilitarian-looking concrete and glass building. No one was in sight, and as Anna paid the driver in traveler's checks and told him to keep the excessive change, he grinned and chattered something profusely in Hebrew. Then he drove off, leaving her with her luggage outside the front door.

She felt a spreading silence resonating from the great expanse of the vast salt sink hole behind her, the Dead Sea, so she turned her attention back to the building, quiet as well, but at least holding promise of life. On entering the dark cave of the building, she found one young Israeli woman, black-haired, down the cool hallway and announced who she was and that she was looking for Nir Teztlah. The young lady informed her, in heavy but correct English, that he was out with a group on a hike, and that Anna had been assigned room 23 at the end of the hall. She pulled some white towels from behind the counter, found the room key, and took Anna to the small, neatly made-up and practical dormitory-style room.

Anna had hoped for better accommodations, but when she put her bag down on the bed and went to open the glass doors leading on to the porch, she saw that she came out to a view over a small canyon that dipped down below her and was filled with palm and date and fig trees, reedy grasses, and rock carved eons ago by water coursing through in flash floods and spring rains.

"Wadi David," said the Israeli girl, pronouncing it "Wah-dee Dah-veed."

"It's . . . stunning," managed Anna.

"Nir hikes there with students today," she told Anna. "He will return to dinner with you. In the dining hall," and she pointed across the room back through the door leading into the hallway. "Just go out the door at the end. You will see it. Dinner is at six o'clock. Enjoy your stay."

Anna thanked her, poured a glass of water from the tap, and went to sit out on the balcony to absorb the view and salt air. She tried conceiving of the land's age, this land that was part of the cradle of civilization, but couldn't quite grasp it. Instead, she decided to listen to the swallowing silence of wilderness. No birds, no lions, no camels, no fluttering of leaves in the trees as in Madison. The palm trees looked as if they were wax and could have been placed there centuries ago. Surely she would be able to at least hear lizards moving under rocks.

Then it occurred to her that she would have to climb higher up the wadi to find a trickle of water, but looking at the clock, she opted instead for reviewing her agenda and then a nap.

She had just finished looking over the rock routes at the Jerusalem site used by local climbers when she heard children's voices bubbling, coming down out of the wadi. Colors dotted with mostly black and brown hair appeared, moving and skipping down the rocks, spilling out a punctuated language she did not comprehend except for its pleasure and excitement. What wonders would the children have discovered on their hike? What stories of each other did they pass around, and were Israeli children any kinder to one another than American children?

Thankfully, she watched them pile into another dormitory building; she anticipated wanting to get a lot of sleep while she was here, and already felt her jet lag.

The children appeared to be on their own as a group, until Anna looked back up into the wadi and saw a lithe, strong-profiled man in sturdy sandals and carrying a small back pack come hopping from stone to stone back down into the school's grounds. His curling dark brown hair was tied back in a messy ponytail, and his forearms, she noticed, were muscular, like a climber's, his belly taut and bronzed. He pulled out his water bottle and she watched his Adam's apple swallow large gulps. Wiping his mouth, he looked up towards her balcony, feeling someone was watching him, and waved with a big grin when he saw his guest had arrived. She returned the wave, smiling tentatively. It would have been better if her host hadn't been so good looking. This was a professional engagement.

Nir disappeared into the building where the children had gone, and Anna decided to take a shower before dinner and read a little.

Anna and Nir met one another formally in the noisy cafeteria with children jostling and jabbering around them. Now he was clean and fresh-smelling, in a colorful cotton short-sleeved shirt; she was momentarily glad she had put on the one skirt she had packed. They both had to raise their voices to hear one another above the clamor.

"You had a safe flight, I take it?" He stuck out his large and welcoming grip, encompassing her hands in both of his.

"Fine, thanks. It's a long flight, though, and you'll probably lose me pretty soon tonight. How do you see the day going tomorrow?"

"I thought we could meet around ten-thirty in the morning, give you some time to get up and adjust. It usually takes about four days to totally adjust, but of course we need to begin our work before then. I thought tomorrow we could go over our gear systems and operating policies, and then you could join me for a small hike up the wadi, if you are not too tired. Then we'll have Sabbath off, and Sunday we'll head to Jerusalem to plan out the site."

"Sounds great." Most of Anna's energy was going towards smiling, showing her white, American, orthodontured teeth, trying to make a good impression, because she was growing wearier by the minute and didn't have much else to give.

After a meal of institutional humus, pita bread, falafel, and a chopped tomato and cucumber salad, and small talk about climbing at Devil's

Lake, Anna took her tray to the cleaning window and dropped her fork and knife into the bucket of soapy water.

"I'm sorry, you'll have to excuse me—I'm really flagging. See you in the morning?"

Nir put out his big paw to touch her shoulder, hair wild about him, looked into her eyes, and said with compassion, "Sleep well. Dream deeply—Wadi David and the Dead Sea air come together and provide people with wonderful dreams. See you in the morning."

Curling up in her bed alone like a child, the still and quiet black air of the desert expanding in the sky outside her window, Anna fell asleep with the feel of Nir's hand on her shoulder.

17

"THERE'S A PROFOUND SILENCE in the City of Rocks in Idaho," Anna intoned to Nir as they trekked up the wadi. They were now about forty-five minutes away from the school.

"Like the silence here, it sounds like," said Nir.

The day had started cool and cloudy, with the possibility of thunderstorms forming later, so they had spent a quick morning going over the belaying practices the school used, the typical populations the school worked with, and its institutional gear. Anna had recommended some updating of some of the equipment and the belaying teaching method. Afterwards, Nir had offered to take Anna up into the inner folds of the desert oasis, warning her that they might have to turn back if it looked like rain. And so they were cautiously wending their way up the ever-narrowing, undulating rock bed formed by rains that could flash-flood in minutes if the conditions were right. Pockets and pools of stagnant water stood in carved-out potholes, and occasionally a lizard darted from shade to shade.

"The rock here is not good, it is like, it's something like you say, a frying pan?"

She laughed and said "Friable. It's friable. Rotten. Crumbles like feta cheese under your hands."

"Yes, yes, goat cheese. No good for climbing."

"Not if you want to have a family and a normal life. Do you have a family?" she queried him.

He was slow to respond.

"I did. But the boy lives with his mother, in Sfed, a pretty little town farther north and west of us here."

"Oh, I'm sorry. I didn't mean to pry."

"It's all right," he glanced back at her. "I see my son a few times a year, and we have as good a relationship as can be expected."

"How old is he now?"

"He'll be twelve. His mother and I were divorced when he was two, so he doesn't remember us being together. I think it's better that way for the children when it happens. Besides, she has a boyfriend now. The boy is attached to him." They picked their way among rocks and boulders that choked up a smaller and smaller stream bed.

"What's his name? Your son, I mean."

"Duvid."

"Is that David? Like the wadi?"

"Yes, the Yiddish form, after my grandfather, who died at Auschwitz. Tradition has us name our children after relatives who have died, rather than relatives who are still living. Superstition, I think."

Anna was quiet as she took all this in. She had never spoken to anyone who had been affected by the Holocaust, and she wasn't quite sure how to respond without embarrassing herself.

"Have you been to Yad Vashem?" she asked.

"Yes, yes, you should go if you get the chance. Perhaps while we're in Jerusalem you will have time on an afternoon. Especially you should see the children's memorial, and the photographs of the Warsaw ghetto."

"I'm a little frightened to go see it—I think I might be over-whelmed."

He stopped hiking and looked back at her, admiring her openness about such a vulnerability.

"It will be all right. It is all, ah, tastefully, I guess, done. If you can call it that. Nothing to fear. Yes, it will stir up feelings, but that is as it should be. It's easy to come and look at modern Israel and simply see us as another contemporary society, technological and fast-paced just like every developed country in the world. But our history does render us distinct, as does our precarious existence here," he said as he smiled at her and offered her a drink of water from his plastic water bottle.

They were within close proximity, and as she wiped the water droplets from the corner of her mouth, she caught his working scent, his olive skin glistening. They each laughed a little and looked down at their feet.

"Well, I thought we would find water sooner today," he said, squinting up into the changing sky. "But at least you get to see the beauty of the canyon within the desert surrounds. So now we can head back. And after tomorrow we will climb together in Jerusalem!"

His words broke a sweet unease between them, and she stepped back some, admiring the sinuous rock formations pushing out their surrounding greenery. But the clouds were thickening and darkening, so Nir told her they should turn around.

"And you? Are you—I think Americans say, attached? Do you have children?"

"Only those I teach to climb, and the mustangs I work with," and sometimes Jonathan, she thought, but leaving him out because of the dissonance under which they had parted, though she didn't feel quite right that she was leaving out mention of him.

They began to talk of the horses, then got into a who's who of climbs they'd done, places they'd climbed, and people they'd climbed with, but it was a friendly one-upsmanship, unlike most of the scrabbling résumé comparisons she got into with other male climbers, who always seemed to have a hard time respecting how much she'd climbed, how good she was, and how many bodies she'd rescued from climbs gone wrong.

Just then a crack of lightning blazoned the sky and they both began counting. Six seconds and they both knew the storm was right above them, so Nir grabbed Anna by the elbow and began herding her back down the wadi.

"We have to get out of here! If it floods and we are caught in it, it won't be good."

A small trickle of water began following them, its tongue growing larger, then turning brown and frothy in a silt and air mix. Soon they were wading through a living puddle, slipping and getting drenched in the rain that was now a downpour. They made it to the mouth of the wadi just as a small stream had formed, and Nir told her this would grow to a torrent within minutes. They just made it out, panting and soaked, hair straggling down their faces.

Anna and Nir slopped in their sandals back to the buildings, coming to Anna's hall, and Nir escorted her to her door. She paused and turned to him as he hung his hand on the door lintel, leaning above her.

"I do have a sort of a boyfriend," she began uncomfortably.

"Ah . . ."

"We're not really on good terms right now," she was surprised to hear herself say. "But . . ."

"Your trip is a business trip. It's best to keep business as business, don't you agree?" He straightened up and faced her.

"Yes. I wouldn't want the Ein Gedi school to find me unprofessional."

"Right. Then, tomorrow evening is Sabbath. You can watch a belay instruction session in the morning, and I go to the Galil to spend it with my family. I would invite you . . ."

"That's quite all right. Thank you for the tour today." She became stiff and formal. "So, then, Sunday—"

"Sunday we'll go to Gai ben Hinom. We'll get settled in to Jerusalem at my friend's and then check out the climbing site. You have the route descriptions?" He was making as much small talk as he could.

"Yes."

"Good. We'll leave at 8:00 on Sunday." He pursed his lips at her. "Shabbat Shalom."

"Uh, yeah, uh, same to you . . ." But he had already turned and was headed down the hallway.

Anna spent her Friday afternoon and Saturday catching up on the last bit of jet lag. The entire school had emptied Friday afternoon, kids departing and staff going to join family as a peace more somnolent than usual settled over the Dead Sea, and Saturday morning she had slept in. The negative elevation must have pulled her down into dreams, because she woke, napped, woke, ate some sandwiches pre-made for the day of rest, napped and dreamed again, wrote in her journal, called Jonathan but reached his voicemail, and sat out on the porch watching the sky glow orange with the setting sun. Time suspended itself here in this land set aside for the Sabbath, reminiscent of God in the silence. She pondered all this in her heart, and wondered if perhaps a single full day like this was, in fact, enough to rejuvenate a person.

Sunday morning, Anna was caught up on her sleep and felt within her own skin again. Nir came to find her after breakfast, and they greeted each other with a general feeling of well-being after polite inquiry about one another's Sabbath rest.

"I thought we could load gear into the van, and head over to my friend's house this morning. We'll have lunch with him and perhaps his wife, then head out to Gai ben Hinom in the afternoon just to have a first look at it."

Anna was agreeable, so they went to the storeroom at the end of the children's building and loaded the multicolored perlon ropes and the rack of gear and webbing into an old van with partially working and noisy air conditioning. Nir began humming "Good morning beautiful, how was your night/Mine was wonderful with you by my side," and Anna looked at him sidelong, wondering what on earth he was thinking.

As they wound their way through the Judean desert in the van, making the climb to Jerusalem, they came across a Bedouin market set up along the road.

"Here, let's take a look at this. I think it'll be an experience for you," said Nir. He had about run out of questions to ask Anna about horses and the rock gym.

They parked the car, cracking open a couple of windows to let out some of the blistering heat. Nir steered Anna toward some tables set up with handmade, deeply dyed and highly colored crafts. Dark-skinned and magnificent-nosed Bedouin in dust-covered robes, heads wound in cloth, converged on them, a few at a time speaking rapid-fire Arabic with hands waving, intending to entice Nir and Anna into buying every item on display at every booth.

"Lo, lo," Nir said simply, waving them off, until they began falling off like flies battered into listlessness by the baking sun. He kept his hand on Anna's arm, a protective gesture for which she was grateful at this point, and invited her to look at a particular table that displayed small round mirrors encased by an embroidered padding that had a small rectangle with a silver spout at the top. Anna stared at a series of them strung together, finding them outlandish and beautiful at the same time, then she began to reach out to touch one.

A particularly tiny Bedouin trader with a too-large headpiece lit upon her, grinning and chattering away in a tongue she couldn't decipher but nonetheless got the gist of. She was really interested in the entire string, but what she came away with was one that he pulled apart from the whole series, so she pulled out some shekels and settled for the single mirror. Nir and Anna kept moving, and she quickly understood that anything she should turn her attention to would draw droves of traders in her direction, so she attached herself to Nir more firmly, kept her mouth shut, and moved quickly taking in as much of the visual potpourri as she could.

A booth with long black dresses swirling with brilliant magenta embroidery caught her eye, and she found herself smiling at one dress in particular, so she reached out to feel the fabric. This was a mistake. A small-statured trader with long and gnarled fingers came out from behind the booth to begin the rush of words convincing her of the item's superior quality, the steadfastness of the dye, and so on, all of which she sort of but did not really understand. She let go and shook her head, saying "Lo, lo," as Nir had taught her, and showed the man that she only had a few shekels in her hand. The trader became offended. His language sped up, and he pushed the dress in her direction. She indicated no with her head more firmly, looking him in the eye, saying the Hebrew words for no again, but this was a mistake as well. He shook the dress at her, bellowed, pointed at the dress, and then at her. His eyebrows took on a life of their own, and Anna turned with a helpless look to Nir. He winced, and repeated what Anna had said, adding in Hebrew that they were not interested.

The Bedouin "bah!"ed and nearly spat at Anna's feet, then turned on his heel to go back behind his booth. Nir and Anna began to slink away, thinking they were free, when the trader turned on them again and lunged after them, grabbed the shekels out of Anna's hand, shoved the dress at her, and cursed under his breath.

"Come on, let's go," Nir directed, and led Anna away from the trader's zone.

"But I didn't want the dress!"

"Yes, I know, but it doesn't work that way here. You bargain. The trader will give you the item for dirt rather than let you go away with nothing. It's just the way it works."

"But what if I don't want it?"

"It's just the way it works," he shrugged helplessly. "Don't you bargain in America?"

"No means no!" she fired back. "If you don't want something, you don't buy it. And the price is the price! On almost everything."

"Well, the character of the people here is different. They are passionate. About everything."

"I guess," she said, folding the dress and putting it on top of the climbing gear.

Under his breath Nir muttered, "It's not such a bad thing," and they began winding their way again to Jerusalem.

18

NIR HAD DRIVEN ANNA and the loaded-up van onto a ridge of West Jerusalem to the house of his friend, which was perched on a hill and drenched in bougainvillea. Nir's friend was still at work, but his friend's wife, Vivian, a blonde-haired, blue-eyed Jew from the northern mountainous region of Italy, showed them their rooms in the tile-floored house, and they got settled in. Vivian tried to keep in check her three young boys as they tore about the house playing after school. A Palestinian housekeeper from East Jerusalem hosed the tile floor down into its drain in the center of the living room, then left for home in the afternoon.

After a glowing evening of good company and Mediterranean dinner after Jeff, Vivian's husband, got home, Anna excused herself early and fell off to sleep.

Anna woke, disoriented. She looked out over the dawning of Jerusalem and did some stretching, watching the growing pink as the night blue disappeared from the sky. The city was both ancient and modern, layered in tiers like a wedding cake from all the conquests and reconstruction over centuries and millennia. Walking quietly out onto the cool tile floor into the central atrium of the house, she looked up and saw the three boys tumbled together on the top mattress of a bunk bed set in a loft, and smiled at the seemingly normal existence in this place that was as politically, militarily, religiously, and historically layered as it was archeologically.

Smelling coffee, Anna went towards the back of the house and found Vivian in her robe, making pancakes. Anna said good morning, headed to the shower, and bumped into Nir in his boxer shorts on the way. He smiled his good morning and stepped out of her way, but not fast enough for her not to take in his sleepy but athletic frame.

After breakfast, Vivian packed lunches for the two of them, and they departed with the gear to take the bus for some sight-seeing, giving the rock a chance to warm up before their work got underway.

Jerusalem was a modern city, like any other in some ways, but vastly different from anything Anna had seen before. People used laptops and iPods on the bus, but on every bus there were also soldiers, young men and women alike, dressed in uniform and carrying automatic weapons. Anna wasn't sure if she should feel safe or threatened. Nir explained to her that before the events in Gaza, there had been some incidents of young, economically disenfranchised East Jerusalemite backhoe drivers who would simply lose control and plow into traffic, killing and injuring Israelis. Those Israelis who had put in their two or three years of required service to the military still were allowed to carry weapons, so there was always a sort of presence, a guardianship, reminding people they lived in a military state. Anna wondered if she had been a Palestinian if she would have felt like she imagined the American colonists felt when they had had English soldiers in their midst.

The bus dropped Anna and Nir near Yad Vashem, the Holocaust museum, and they walked past bustling Israelis who struck Anna, on the whole, as short on civility, to the point of being rude at times. Perhaps living under the gun removed social niceties, she thought. They walked past shops and bakeries with the strange Hebrew lettering on storefronts, and Anna glanced at newspaper stands, taking in the foreign words with photos. Cedar trees yearned upwards, as if drawn by tornado force, pointing towards heaven at their tops. The stone of the city was pink and dusted gold, the streets either ancient cobbled or modern asphalt, and green abounded—not damp and lush, but intentional, like so many golf courses in the desert flats of Nevada. Even most of the flowers were more defensive than delicate and moist.

Because the land did not feel mossy, like Madison, Anna turned her attention more to the architecture, trying to grasp the contrast between aged stone blocks piled on by hands and backs long dead amidst clean glass and concrete moved by diesel-powered Mercedes machines.

Nir told Anna he had a meeting at the five-star King David Hotel and would be back to fetch her in a couple of hours.

"You'll probably want about two hours here—any more can get to be too much. See you in a while then?"

She thanked him, and reluctantly went in to purchase her ticket. Washington, D.C.'s Holocaust Memorial Museum had left her in a disembodied mental state for several hours afterwards, so she wasn't sure it was such a good idea to visit Yad Vashem before trying to put up routes in the afternoon.

She made her way through the stark displays, most of which were photos in black and white with odd descriptions at the bottom of each. Her feet grew tired as she looked at the photos closely.

Then, on rounding a corner, she saw Edna sitting, alone, on the one utilitarian bench the museum seemed to have provided in the entire place. She was sitting before a photo of the Warsaw Ghetto, in which a man in a wool overcoat, hat on his head, was stepping around an emaciated woman wearing a cotton print dress who lay in a fetal position on a sidewalk. Other people on the street continued about their business as well, and in the background there were others, a couple of children, also lying starving on the pavement.

Anna was off to Edna's side and slightly behind her. The ceiling light for the photo cast a darkness behind Edna, but provided enough illumination for Anna to see that Edna was sitting ram-rod straight, wide awake, and a line of dried tears had run down into her ear. Her chin was puckered. Anna's mouth opened momentarily and she took a step forward, but then frowned and turned around. She left Edna sitting by herself and went into another room.

It occurred to her that she had as much trouble trying to grasp the idea of how the Holocaust could have happened as she did the concept of the Holy Trinity, which evaded her and made no rational sense. The magnitude of each defied not just the mind, but the depths of human emotion, it seemed to her. It was as if the only way to comprehend either would have been to have lived in the era itself, to have been a Jew of the Holocaust, or, conversely, a disciple—or at least to have known one, or known Jesus himself.

She went outside to find the children's memorial and felt the live air on her face. Jerusalem presented itself to her as a ghost of this dilemma: clearly, the layers of the city testified to its existence in the dawning Christian era, and before. The rock she would climb was older than human history. Natural features and human history had never been so entwined for her; she shuddered, and thought that perhaps this visceral connection through the natural world was the only way for her to deeply imagine the sufferings of human beings over time. Maybe Edna grasped that depth in another way.

Nir had come back, and he could see the gap of understanding in her dazed look.

"Why don't we head for the climbs now? It's quite a lot to take in all in one morning, and it would be nice for me to have you somewhat present for what we're about to do!"

"That's fine. I'm full up. And getting hungry, too."

"Okay, we'll eat on the bus."

They heaved the backpacks up on their shoulders again and made their way toward the bus that would take them to the Valley of ben Hinom, Gehenna.

"In earliest times, this valley used to be a burning garbage dump. And way back, from the first Temple period, supposedly the pagans burned children in sacrifice to the god Moloch. So it doesn't have a good reputation. You've probably heard of Jesus threatening to send sinners to Gehenna, to outer hell. None of this area was built up, until fairly recently, in fact." He gestured to the New City, the valley outside the southern wall of the Old City, which had filled with modern construction. "All that Gehenna means is Valley of the son of Hinom. I have no idea who Hinom was." As Nir sat next to Anna on the bus seat she felt the hairs on his forearm just tickling the skin of her arm, and the sensuousness brought her acutely back into her body after the museum experience. Surely he had to be as aware of this contact as was she.

She nodded at what Nir said and looked around, confused as to where they were in the modern, upscale, contorted-pattern neighborhoods. She was used to the grid-pattern of counties and farms and streets in the Midwest, which looked from a plane like a patchwork quilt, orderly.

The bus dropped them a few blocks from their destination, and they hoisted their backpacks to walk the remaining distance. Unfamiliar and pleasant smells wafted on the breeze as Anna wondered what layers of old neighborhoods and artifacts she walked upon. She could understand why being an archeologist here might be very exciting.

As they neared the wall of the Old City they walked past the Jerusalem Cinematheque, home of the Jerusalem film festival, Nir informed Anna. As they approached the crag, a dog ran by barking at them.

"Do dogs just run loose here? And are we likely to encounter any other climbers today?" she asked Nir.

"Well, they're not supposed to. And possibly, to your second question, but since it's in the middle of a workday, probably not. In any case, there are plenty of climbs here. Everything is one pitch, and the harder routes are bolted. Of course the school won't be using those so much. What I've gotten permission for is to bolt some of the easier routes at the top, because otherwise we'd have to set up all the climbs we'd use with protection, and, as you know, it's just safer for us to rely on the bolts than the expertise of the climbing instructors getting the protection right one hundred percent of the time. Sad, but true. Israel is not exactly the place in the world churning out a high number of radical climbers, so we focus more on the interpersonal qualities of the instructors instead of their technical expertise."

"Makes perfect sense. And whatever you and I can do to make the systems bombproof—oh, sorry, maybe you don't use that phrase here?" she said, embarrassed.

"No, no, that's fine, I've climbed around enough to know what you mean," he said, laughing.

They stopped at the base of the cliff and put down the packs. Anna found comfort in knowing the rock had been there longer than even the wall, and she walked up close and put a hand on the limestone, feeling its coolness even in the growing heat of the day. It had a slight earthy-metallic smell to it, and she felt its substantial friction surface under her fingers. Rubbing her fingers together, she turned to Nir, smiled, and said, "Let's get to it, then!"

Nir showed her the range of climbs, crack systems and friction-face, as they walked along the base to a crumbled weak area, which was the access scramble route to the top of the climbs. Once on top, they looked out over the neighborhoods in the Valley of Hinom, feeling the quiet of this area, which had a shortened golf-course type of grass struggling up amongst the pathways at the bottom, as if nibbling sheep were herded through often. Anna looked about and smelled the wind again, as if it swirled currents from the Dead Sea miles away and also the olive trees from the Mount of Olives. No hint of burning garbage dump lingered. It was beautiful in an austere, pinched way, and Anna reflected on some of the dramatic vistas she had looked out upon from the tops of cliffs. The view was actually one of the peak reasons she climbed, though few people besides Jonathan knew it.

They picked their way over to one of the larger hand-crack systems, and Anna examined the bare top of the climb. There were easy bolt placements, so she marked them with some chalk to come back to tomorrow when Nir was gone and she could take her time drilling in the bolts. But as they worked for the afternoon, she described to him the tremors at Devil's Lake, and he told her of some of the climbing in Greece he had done recently at the rock formations in a small, cloistered town that had high up on its cliffs an ancient monastery, accessible only by basket on a cable strung high above the valley.

The tensions of their mutual attraction Anna and Nir placed aside during the time they were working together; they got in sync and handled the ropes and gear effortlessly. Clearly they were a good team, communicating well from top to bottom as they ticked off the sample climbs that would be suitable for students. The afternoon wound down the clock, and soon they saw the setting sun glowing behind the western walls of the Old City. A light breeze drifted across the valley, as sensuous on Anna's skin as the hairs from Nir's forearm had been.

Soon it was time to return, and they packed up everything they had come with except a few ropes left set up on a couple of climbs they had not gotten to. Anna would return on her own first thing in the morning and use a jumar, a piece of equipment that would allow her to solo climb while at the same time belay herself. Nir had to return that night to Ein Gedi for a new group coming in next morning, so he drove her back to Vivian and Jeff's.

As they said goodbye to one another, promising to meet up in two days, Nir took Anna's hand and gallantly kissed the back of it like a suitor from another time. She looked down at the ground, wishing in a fantastical moment that things might be otherwise in her love life, then shook Nir's hand awkwardly in goodbye. He crossed the stone pavement, got into the aged van, and drove off, leaving Anna to a peaceful evening of watching *The Goofy Movie* with Jeff and Vivian and their children. She waited to call Jonathan somewhat later because of the time difference, but she also delayed because she wanted to preserve the feeling of the day for herself.

When she did call, he sounded groggy and grumpy.

"Hey."

"Hey, luv. What's happening?"

He paused, and sighed.

"Look, I've got some bad news for you. My niece, you know, Tina, died in a motorcycle accident two nights ago."

Anna sat, stunned, then babbled out a torrent of questions.

"What do you mean? What happened? She was engaged, wasn't she? Why didn't you call me? Oh, Jonathan, how sad. When is the funeral? Do you want me to come home?"

"Anna, Anna, slow down. No, I—I don't want you to come all the way back for this. The funeral is Wednesday. They don't know exactly what happened, but she was riding her motorcycle to work to save on gas, and it looks like she took an exit too fast and maybe changed her mind at the last minute. There was no one else involved. Dan, her fiancé, missed her because she was late getting home from work, and then he heard about a crash on highway 51, and next thing a state trooper showed up at his door to tell him. He got to see her body after they cleaned it up a little, and then they had her cremated. It's so terribly sad," he said, pressed down upon with the grief. "I miss you," he added.

"Oh God, Jonathan, Oh God," she said. She paced the floor and wiped her hand across her face and nose, crying. "I should be there with you. I know I should be there."

Jonathan was quiet, then said, "There's nothing you could do. I'll let people know you're out of the country. Again." He didn't mean to thump the last word, and instantly regretted it.

Anna sat helplessly on the floor and cried some more into the phone, heartsick.

"I'm so sorry I'm not there. Oh, Jonathan, I don't know what to do."

"There's nothing you can do. We just have to ride it out. But look, I'm pretty beat and I need to catch up on some sleep. Let's talk later, maybe after the funeral, okay?"

"Okay," she said in a small voice.

19

ANNA WOKE AGAIN EARLY, this time interrupting her dream of Nir calling from a cliff top like a mullah at prayer in the late afternoon hours, with the sun setting in one part of the sky and the moon rising in the other. A sea of emaciated creatures swam beneath him, mummified, it seemed, and she woke in a sweat, mildly frightened, her eyelids swollen from crying the night before.

Walking into the kitchen she came upon Vivian, also up early after a disturbed night of Jeff kicking and thrashing in their bed. Anna told Vivian about Jonathan's niece, and her work with autistic kids, and how she had been going to get married the next April. Vivian was sympathetic.

"It's so hard, with tragedies like that. It's worse when someone is young, because it's not just the present that's been lost, but the future of that person's life as well. We're so invested in the lives of our young people. I'm sure Jonathan's doing his best right now. And we'll say some prayers for the whole family."

"I really appreciate your being able to let me stay with you," Anna said.

"Oh, I'm glad it worked out. That's the way people do it here. It's one of the things I was drawn to the most when I considered moving here."

"When did you make . . . is it, *aliyah*?" Anna asked, referring to the term for immigration of diaspora Jews to the homeland of Israel.

"In '94. After Jeff's brother had. Because his parents were both gone, it didn't make sense for him to stay in the States. Not that we had no reservations about coming here—life is much more tenuous in a lot of ways. Water is a real issue, and I'm still not used to that. And we are poised on the brink of war at all times. In some ways it's a trauma-filled existence, and that's not even taking into consideration how it is for the Palestinians. But it was the right decision, and now I can't imagine going back."

"And now your children don't know any different, do they?"

"No, except that they have been to the States a few times to visit Grandma and Grandpa, my parents. If you consider Florida the States, anyway," she said, laughing. "How do you like it so far?" she looked at Anna quizzically.

Anna considered a diplomatic response. "It strikes me as very ancient, but in a way I can't quite grasp, because I don't know much of the history of the area, and although there are ancient buildings here, the place is so modern you could come here as an alien and almost think the ancient structures are just oddly out of place. I get the feeling most people here are bonded to the earth in some sort of long, invisible chain, which anybody other than Jews and Arabs will have a hard time comprehending. The modern people do seem a little, um, hustled and hurried . . ."

"You mean nasty and short?" Vivian interjected as Anna searched for words.

"Well, yeah, sort of. I thought Americans were impolite!"

"No, Americans are just loud compared to other people!" Vivian laughed.

They finished their coffee, having enjoyed the quiet talk in the early morning hours. Then Anna prepared to go back to the climbing area.

"Be careful," said Vivian, as she brought Anna out a homemade sack lunch of humus and tabouleh and pita, along with copious water. "You have to drink a lot in the desert here, and you have to watch out for the bats."

"The bats?"

"Yes, they say there are bats in some of the cracks of the climbs at Gai ben Hinom. Just thought you should know. You don't want to dig too deeply into the cracks. Sometimes they live in there. You want to avoid getting bitten and having to get rabies shots."

Anna walked, a stranger in a strange land, finally with some time alone. She passed by more pointed cedars and hedges of fragrant bougainvillea. It was still early, and the ropes she and Nir had set the previous day still hung there, untouched. Ruminating about Tina and Jonathan and barely paying attention to what was around her, she set aside the small pack with her harness, chalk bag, shoes, lunch, and water, and began doing some warm-up stretches. The same dog came sniffing by, and she shooed it off, hoping her lunch would remain intact while she climbed alone. More than one critter had chewed through packs she had left at the bases of climbs. She ought to get a super-soaker water gun, she thought, and carry it up with her when she soloed. She tied on her shoes and threaded the buckle through on her harness, checking it methodically to make sure she was completely safe. Lyn Hill, world-famous climbing goddess as she was, had mistakenly done up only the first half of her harness thread-through one day, leaned back at the top of a climb, and gone screaming down about fifty feet before grounding, miraculously not seriously injured. Anna wished to avoid such a mistake, especially given that the only one around was the lecherous dog.

Affixing the jumar to the rope, she began climbing the first sweet and easy 5.6 route, one that would be nonetheless challenging for students. When she reached the top she drilled and placed the bolts for the climb, rappelled down, and pulled the rope.

As she started the second climb, different in character but rated the same, Anna felt the limestone under her hands again. She began alternately feeling her way up the rock, then ratcheting the jumar up the fixed rope to arrest herself from falling very far if she should happen to come off. She was good enough so that she could have done the climb without a rope, truly soloing it, but the rope added psychological security. Besides, if she were to fall, the story in the newspaper would look really bad.

About twenty-five feet up she came to a small lip of rock on which she rested her feet, a no-hands hold. She dipped her hand into her chalk bag absent-mindedly and looked out and around, then turned her intense focus back to the rock. She shifted, playing with the angles at this particular resting spot, and turned her body one hundredeighty degrees. Rather than jamming her fist into the crack before her as the climb was probably normally done, from her turned position she used a lay-back technique, sliding her hands deep into the crack and leaning her entire body weight off her straight and weight-loaded arms. All the while she thought of Vivian's bats.

Just then her fingers brushed up against something that moved slightly, so she quickly retreated and took her stance on the small ledge again, heart pounding. She jammed her fist in the way the climb would normally be done, and felt nothing, despite stretching deeply back into the crack. So she turned to repeat the layback move, and when she did, she again just lightly jostled something inserted farther into the crack. It didn't respond like a live creature, so her fear turned to curiosity. Stretching her shoulder joints to elongate them as much as possible, she wiggled her fingers and got the rock or object to move more. Then she heard a clink-chink sound, and she followed the internal crack down its length, coming to rest on a now-loose object.

As if inhaling to fit into a zippered dress just minutely too small for her, she held her breath and again lengthened her arms, and therefore fingers, to begin delicately sliding the object towards her, out of the crack. Finally, she wiggled it forward enough to get a minimal grip on it with her index and middle fingers. Shutting her eyes and willing it forward, she pulled out towards her a small round clay container that was heavy for its size, about five inches long and three-quarters of an inch in diameter. She turned it in her hands, forgetting she was standing on a ledge only about one inch in relief from the rock wall. Looking quizzically at it she opened her chalk bag all the way and slipped the object into it lengthwise. Finishing out the climb, Anna sat at the top, legs dangling off the edge of the rock.

The chalk bag didn't want to release the clay container as readily as it had accepted it, so Anna worked the bag around her harness and unclipped it from its fastening carabiner. But as it slipped and bumped onto the rock surface next to her hip, the clay cracked, breaking off the top stopper. Sand spilled out. Anna picked up the container and pried at the top of it with her fingers, never considering it might be thousands of years old and a protected archeological find. As she poked at the broken clay, more sand leaked out, until Anna could peer inside and see what looked like a piece of paper rolled up.

She stopped and looked up and out furtively, wondering if anyone had seen her, because she began to suspect she had something very old in her hands. Next, she spread the mouth of her chalk bag wide and sprinkled its remaining contents on the wind, sending the white powder drifting over the valley of Hinom. She smacked the chalk bag on the rock to empty it as much as she could, then she put the clay vessel back into the chalk bag, securing the toggle on the chalk bag's drawstring tightly.

Anna hurriedly drilled the bolts for the climb, descended, pulled the rope, and packed up. Wending her way through the neighborhood, she made her way back to Jeff and Vivian's.

Vivian had told Anna she would be out for the day with the children, visiting their aunt and uncle up north, so Anna showered and got herself a snack of persimmons, then settled in to the cool tile-floored house. She unpacked the clay container and ran her hands over it more carefully this time. Pouring out the remaining sand, she gingerly lifted out the scroll. A few remnants of sand fell off it, and with fingers quivering Anna opened the surprisingly sturdy roll. What she saw amazed her.

A few fine pages of what appeared to be a cloth-type of paper were covered in tiny script, Hebrew to her eye, though she couldn't be certain. For a few moments she froze, her eyebrows arched in astonishment. She wasn't sure if she had found something truly ancient and sacred, or a modern young girl's lovesick letter in a bottle, from the feminine look of the hand—or, something altogether different that her imagination could only embellish.

Pacing the floor, Anna periodically looked sideways at the object, uncertain what to do with it. For all she knew, she might have damaged it just by touching it, hell, just from looking at the darn thing. She had heard of the find of the Dead Sea Scrolls nearby, but she had also heard that it was the desert climate that preserved such ancient texts—complete dryness. She thought the more moist climate of Jerusalem—it did rain nearer the Dead Sea, after all—would make it unlikely anything very old would survive centuries of dampness, although it did seem that the item being packed in sand and clay might have survived in its own protected environment. Maybe somewhat like the climate-controlled chambers created for precious artworks and documents, she figured.

Her face worked as she considered her options. No doubt there would be some sort of regulation involving found artifacts, some way of protecting archeological finds. Or perhaps it would be worth money—a lot of money!

The afternoon was descending, and Anna knew Vivian and the children would be back soon, so she carefully packed the paper back in its clay container, filling it with the sand as much as she could. The rest she swept away with a single hand swipe, and the grains disappeared, dispersed across the tile floor of the house, with no one to suspect anything other than dirt tracked in.

I know what I'll do, Anna thought. I'll call Edna and ask her to read it to me, if it is in fact Hebrew. I can trust her. She'll know what it is, and then we can figure out what to do.

20

Jerusalem, 35 C.E.

A VIEL'S HANDWRITING HAD TAKEN on a delicate and distinctive flow as she worked her way from writing in wax pallets to clay to the codex, a form used primarily for business transactions and casual writings. In the privacy of her own room she would work with parchment scrolls, knowing she would never be allowed to scribe a sacred Torah scroll, but she did this for her own practice and simply because she loved the feeling of parchment. When she wrote with this format, mostly in the dawn with her table positioned so she had a view of golden glow of the city out her window, she felt as if she were flying. Her hand moved even faster than it normally did, and she felt tied into the spirit of God in a way she believed few women of her time experienced.

Gradually her script became smaller and smaller and almost perfectly regular. As she wrote, she established a shortened version of some words in order to keep the flow regular and moving quickly. Her hand stopped its tingling and burning, which had increased over time when it was idle. Devising a shortened form of each person's name she wrote, she kept in contact with her sister, Devorah, regularly, and more sporadically her parents. To them she wrote details of her life in Jerusalem, each letter containing some humor, along with the lives in her immediate vicinity—her aunt and uncle, the servants and their families and cares. Rarely did she write about political movements in and around Jerusalem; she was more interested in the earnestness of people's daily lives.

Each personal letter was adorned with elaborate scrollery of her own creation. The missives were sent most often with friends of Mordechai's who were traveling from Jerusalem toward the north. Devorah wrote back most regularly, and she had had four letters from John.

John's passion centered on Yeshua's teachings, his discussions of the coming kingdom of God, and the miracles the rabbi continued to perform. Only in closing did John loosen his heartstrings and include a single paragraph about his ardor for Aviel. On occasion he would write her of his dreams, which she found wildly entertaining and would interpret for him in her response. It was difficult to be so far away and feel so distant from him, but at the same time their exchange of letters was developing as she had hoped—she got to know better the tenor of the young fisherman turned disciple, began to trust his character from the remove of miles and landscape and mission.

Aviel did long for John, but she also knew what he was engaged in was something quite out of the ordinary. She tried to conceive of where it was all leading him, and the group of men following Yeshua; a return to fishing after Yeshua's flame died a natural death seemed most likely to her. And yet the reports they heard back about his growing ministry concerned her because it seemed the flame only grew brighter and would have to be doused at some point by the machine of priesthood and Rome in Jerusalem. If Yeshua stayed in the north, his actions and words would remain inconsequential; it began to seem inevitable that he would come back to the city, but even Mordechai hesitated to forecast what might happen then. Whenever Aviel heard the conversation come up, Mordechai's face grew dark and his brow furrowed, and words died in a hush.

So Aviel had written John and asked him when he would return, and what Yeshua intended.

I hardly know, John had written back. *We travel day to day, listening, eating, and sleeping. It's as if Yeshua is sustained from within and has no bodily needs. He seems to think us weak at times, needing rest and food as we do, though we are only expending ourselves walking, not fishing. My back weakens, but my legs grow stronger. He does eat—I've seen him—but still, at times, he's completely unaware that we—or even he—might need rest and water and food.*

He gives the sense at once of knowing exactly what is coming, and yet at the same time he does not plan from day to day; we merely go. We go. And we minister to the people around us.

On top of that, he has no hesitancy about those from whom we take help and provisions. The elders are scandalized by the people we associate with, as are we, at times. Sometimes I am jealous of the love he shows for prostitutes and the tax collectors, and at other times my heart can go out to them, too.

Yeshua shows us a burning steadiness and an encompassing love and concern, greater than anything described in the scriptures, but at the same time he succumbs to bouts of being temperamental, cursing things in his

*path. But overall, I have never known such a man, and I am in the heart of
his hold.*

When Aviel read these words, she weighed them. And realized she
was loving John all the more for extending himself to discover what the
man Yeshua was.

In the meantime, Devorah had grown older, more shapely, and more ma-
ture, and had asked her mother and father if she could visit her sister in
Jerusalem. Caring for the goats and spinning wool generally contented
her, but she imagined the sights Aviel described and so she wanted to
broaden beyond the small town atmosphere of Capernaum and see the
architecture, market, pools, and olive groves of Jerusalem.

So Devorah arrived with Yohanon and Hepsabah, Yohanon wanting
to come to Jerusalem to sell his tables to other scribes. They came by
donkey and had a long journey of it; Miriam and Mordechai graciously
put them up down the hall from Devorah and Aviel. When Aviel saw
Devorah she ran to greet her, grasping both of her sister's hands in hers,
delight and joyful tears both streaming from her. She clung to Devorah
for a long while, then showed Devorah her room, where a second bed had
been brought in so they could sleep together.

That night, following the recounting of the dry and dusty journey
over dinner, Aviel took Devorah out onto the terrace overlooking the city
as it glimmered to dusk.

"Tell me how *Eemah* and *Abba* are," Aviel begged.

"Well, they are both proud and anguished when they read your letters, they miss you so much. Mother is older—fine lines around her face,
but she still works very hard every day with the animals and garden. Her
feet trouble her sometimes now, but Abba will rub them for her with some
oil, and she likes that."

"And Nabby?"

"Still that strange combination of slow and ornery. He is less toler-
ant of the little boys in the town, and he kicked out at one of them just
recently. Abba had to hit him, and he squealed—it was hard to see. But
otherwise he's okay."

"And what about you?"

They turned from the twilight and began coming back down the
torch-lit corridor to their bedroom.

"I'm well . . ." Devorah smiled a furtive smile, teasing Aviel.

"What? What is it? Are you engaged?"

"Soon to be!" and she burst out laughing.

"Who is it? Who is he? Who has *Abba* chosen for you?"

"Well, you know, really it was *Eemah*—you know how that goes—I heard them talking one night, and I like the choice . . ."

"Who is it?" Aviel nearly leapt upon her sister.

"Samuel, the son of Joseph the water skin maker. Just up the street."

As Aviel sifted the information, she found a hair brush and began brushing out Devorah's long dark hair. Devorah crossed her legs comfortably on the bed and began rattling off Samuel's virtues, including that he had never lost a sheep, knew how to help his father with the wineskins, and had grown two inches just in the last year. He wasn't the handsomest young man, but he was sturdy, and Devorah liked him a great deal, having grown up so close.

"Of course," she added tentatively, "he is second cousin to Nathan."

Aviel's eyes darkened at the memory, but she continued stroking her sister's hair and dismissed any concern, saying, "Well, the town is small, and practically anybody of marriageable age will be related to Nathan somehow. But I know Samuel is a good boy—good man, I mean. I like the match," she pronounced, as if it were her decision to make.

"Oh, Aviel, I want so very much to be married tomorrow! And to live right next door to *Eemah* and *Abba*, and have a house and children—you will have nieces and nephews—and I want you to dress me for my wedding, in all the finery of Jerusalem. Can we go look tomorrow at the souk at fabrics and jewelry?" She could barely contain her enthusiasm, having dreamt and imagined colored silk and embroidery and gold bangles and finely tooled leather sandals for months now.

"Of course! Of course. We'll do the shopping for Aunt Miriam, and you will get to see all there is available. If you can't get it in Jerusalem, trust me, you can't get it anywhere. Except maybe in Rome. But I don't think so. And I'll show you the Temple, of course, too."

They pushed their separate beds together and lay down, but were nowhere near ready to sleep.

"What about you and John?" Devorah asked her sister.

Sighing, Aviel said she had an occasional letter from him, but she really didn't know where he was at any point, though the household heard rumors from travelers coming through and reporting to Mordechai the movements and news-making activities of the prophet who continued to agitate.

"Look, here is my diary. Some of it I extract and put in my letters to John," said Aviel.

Devorah marveled at the fineness of the script, the flourishes and beautiful embellishments.

"Do you do this in all that you write?"

"No, not in the business transactions, like the books that Aunt Miriam gives me to copy. But in personal letters I've been doing for people, yes. They like it—it gives more of a grace and personal touch to the words."

"But some of this is so small I can barely read it! What's this? This word with the line over it?"

"*Abba*! It's a short way of writing '*Abba*.' I made it up myself. And I have symbols I use for 'of,' 'the,' and so on—words I use a lot. When I write John, I shorten Yeshua's name by using just the first two letters of his name. That's a pretty common tradition the scribes have, in Greek especially. Did you know those first two letters equal eighteen, according to the numerical value given to the letters?"

"You mean gematria?" Devorah referred to the practice of assigning numbers to letters, adding them up, and correlating the meaning of the word with the number.

"Yes, sort of, but I don't know a lot about gematria."

"Do you do it in all three languages, Aramaic, Greek, and Hebrew as well?"

"Mostly just in the Aramaic and Greek. I showed my abbreviations to Uncle Mordechai once, a passage I copied from the Torah, actually, and he got angry with me, so I stopped using them for the Hebrew. I was making up my own shortened versions of 'Adonai' and just some other words and he didn't like it, because there are already set forms the Torah scribes use, of course. But mostly I write in Greek, anyway. Except to John. Every once in a while I'll write in Aramaic," and here her eyes turned glassy as she recalled the feel of his hands in hers.

Devorah was stunned by the breadth of her sister's knowledge.

"Do you think there is any chance for you and John to, to . . ." and Devorah trailed off, because she didn't know how to even conceive of completing the thought.

Aviel sighed.

"You know, it's so tangled. I know he is bound to Yeshua. But he says he wants to be with me, as well. That's just not feasible; you and I both know that. I have no idea where this is all taking him, and neither does he. And I think," here she stumbled, "I don't think Yeshua knows some of the time, either," not entirely sounding convinced of her statement.

"You don't think Yeshua knows he's the Son of God?"

"I didn't say that. I think he does know that part. It's just that I don't think Yeshua knows how this is all going to come out. I think he's willing for it to come out however it does, but that certainly leaves a lot of people up in the air. Including John. And that makes him not a very good candidate for a husband." The sadness was evident in Aviel's voice.

"Besides," she added, "I can't have children anyway."

"What do you mean? You mean you still haven't started yet?"

"No. Not once. It's not even erratic. It just hasn't happened. And I don't think it's going to. So Yeshua gave me life a second time, but I can't pass it on. How ironic, don't you think? That a woman—and I'm not even a woman, actually—can live, but only for herself."

Devorah looked at her sister sadly, and took her hand.

"It'll start sometime, Aviel—it has to. It just has to." But she could think of nothing more comforting to say in the face of her sister's barrenness.

"It's a strange death, before my time, to not be able to have children. And yet I live with it. Well, I've gotten used to it. Let's go to bed. It's already late, and the birds call out early here."

They lay down side by side, their arms intertwined, and fell off to sleep under the watch of the sparkling stars and the dry Jerusalem air.

21

DEVORAH RAN FROM STALL to stall in the market, fingering each gold-embroidered cloth, each deeply dyed silken swatch, all having traveled in camel caravans from distant lands across the wilderness wastes, to be absorbed by the wealthy women and men of the city. Her eyes consumed the fine linens, and Aviel could only wonder if her sister had a knack for fabrics and might trade in them someday. It was good to see her passionate about something, and she found herself daydreaming that perhaps Devorah and her soon-to-be husband might get a start here in Jerusalem, keeping Aviel company.

At noon they headed for the Stoa, to meet Mordechai for a quick meal of goat cheese and bread and olives. The sun blazed down on the white, white marble surrounding them, which still felt slightly cool to the touch when sat upon.

Only slightly late, Mordechai came striding from the direction of the inner temple and greeted the women, all smiles.

"What a hot day!" he exclaimed. "How do you find the marvels of the city, Devorah?"

"It's such a delight! I could see moving here, living here."

"Well, you have an open invitation with us. Now, Aviel, I have news for you. I saw Yeshua this morning, and his entourage . . ."

Aviel felt her heart go still. Was John in the city? She had had no recent correspondence from him saying they were heading back to Jerusalem.

"How do they appear, uncle?"

"Ragged!" He laughed. "And unwashed. Good thing I did not get too close. But I invited them to come for a meal tomorrow night."

"And?" She could not hide the anticipation in her voice.

Mordechai searched her face, bemusement in his.

"They did accept, but did not want to be a burden and so will be staying at John's house while here. Yeshua is under even more heat and scrutiny, and I don't expect his visit this time will be better received than it was last time; if anything, he may encounter more hostility and testing from the elders. The stories we have been hearing are unsettling. I don't think he knows what . . . But I shouldn't trouble you with all this."

Mordechai had seemed to forget he was talking to women, but also seemed to need to talk to someone about the stir the prophet had continued to make.

Aviel was simply looking down at her feet, chewing and swallowing her bread, and Devorah became uncomfortable, not knowing where to take the conversation.

"I really enjoyed seeing and feeling all the fabrics, uncle! They are so varied, so foreign, so . . ." she whirled around in delight, her hands over her head.

"Good! I hope you were able to purchase something to take away with you?"

"A small mantle piece for my mother—she'll like it, I think. And a smaller green-and-gold embroidered fabric to make a bag for myself. It's a vanity, I know, but I couldn't resist, and *Abba* and *Eemah* did give me some money to buy a memento."

"And you, Aviel? Did you purchase anything?"

"Only some more parchment, uncle, and a small clay container to send a letter in. I know I have too many writing indulgences . . ."

"Excellent. You should have your hearts' desires, both of you. Now, what are you going to do this afternoon?" Mordechai put his hand on Aviel's shoulder and roused her from her reverie.

Aviel looked at him, wide eyed. At that moment she existed in two simultaneously occurring worlds as he spoke—the present one that he occupied and that was bound to tactile reality—and the one in her head in which she was recalling the last words John had written her, and the last time he had kissed her. This light tension between the two states was for her more common than people suspected—or so she hoped.

Speaking out of the former state, Aviel responded, "I wanted to take Devorah on a walking tour and show her the city some more, and outside the city walls, actually, perhaps even to the Valley of Hinom, if that's acceptable to you, Uncle."

Mordechai pondered.

"It should be safe enough. Do you have enough water for a dry walk?"

"Yes, I believe so."

"Then go, but be sure to be back early enough to help your aunt with any preparations for Sabbath tonight."

Devorah smiled, and Aviel seemed to come back to the senses in charge of the moment somewhat more; as she released memories her body shifted and her shoulders relaxed. She took Devorah's hand and said, "Let's go then, and leave Uncle to his afternoon."

They took their leave, Aviel glancing back only once, almost unaware she was doing so, to see if she could catch sight of John.

Each city gate had a name, and the one the young women headed for was called the Sheep's Gate because sheep were herded out of the city through it. They passed the sizeable Bethzatha pool, and Devorah could only stare at the blind, lame, and paralyzed who languished there. It was guarded by Roman soldiers, who did look twice at them, but let them pass unobstructed, as if they had a veil of protection cocooning them The women quietly padded down the ancient stone steps, looking up and out at the view of the desert valley that stretched in the distance beyond them. Any moisture was snatched out of the air and quickly taken up above, so they drank repeatedly from the water skin as they walked under the sun. They came to the bottom of the steps and turned along the southern wall, which was a piece with the rock crags behind which this portion of the city sat protected. Stunted trees gasped out an existence in some of the cracks of the rock layered to a hardness greater than the hardest marble the city produced.

At the bottom Aviel and Devorah stood, first looking up at the rock encasement, formidable in the face it presented to the wilderness. Next they turned to gaze out upon the desolate wilderness, a haze off in the distance, the smoldering stench of rubbish piles nearer. People came here to burn their detritus, so Gehenna was both literally and metaphorically a wasteland.

"Putrid!" exclaimed Devorah. "Why did we come here?"

"Because I love the distant view here, and it's quiet, and because I love the rock face. Come over here," she said to Devorah as she stood at the base of a fist-width sized crack mid-way along the cliff. She had both her palms spread wide on the marble façade, feeling it as if it were pulsing underneath her touch.

"It's cool to the touch," said Devorah.

"It always seems to be, no matter how hot the day is."

"Do you come here often?"

"Sometimes—to get some quiet. It's hard to find peace within the city limits, except in the early dawn."

"Is it safe here?" Devorah looked around skeptically, wondering if poor people ever came to scavenge the burning heaps of trash.

"I've never had any concern, but I don't tell Aunt Miriam and Uncle Mordechai I come here. It's not seemly for a young lady. But I love this place, really. There's garbage, yes, but there's solitude, and I treasure that. Some very interesting people come here. And I like the contrast with my life at home."

She paused for a moment.

"They say Yeshua eats with prostitutes and tax collectors, instead of elders and upstanding men like Uncle."

This struck Devorah as a non-sequitur, just another one of Aviel's quirky comments, as if she were in conversation with herself.

"And . . .?"

"Well, his doing that is kind of like this place. Two totally opposite things you wouldn't think should go together."

"Are you going to become a follower of Yeshua too?"

Aviel centered her dark eyes on Devorah. "And what if I did?"

A mild but sickly sweet smell wafted towards them on the hot breeze from one of the burn piles nearby, and a shepherd boy came out of the gate in the distance now, heading southwards with his head down. He carried a clanking bell in his hands and was oblivious to the women's presence.

"What would Abba say? Or Uncle?"

"I haven't gotten that far," admitted Aviel. "It's just something I wonder about. They say women are following Yeshua, and one who was unclean even touched him and was healed—unclean like I was. They say he's challenging the interpretation of the laws without fear of reprisal. That he teaches love, and the coming kingdom of God."

"And what about rebellion? Ousting the Roman army? Would you get mixed up in that? Or are you just interested in what he's doing, for John's sake?" Devorah did not hide her concern.

"Politics I don't give a fig about. That's the concern of men, and all they do is lie. What Yeshua did for me is not a lie. It's as honest and real as anything ever is." The heat in her voice conveyed both her indignation and conviction.

Devorah couldn't follow this new passion of her sister's. It was as if she were thinking ahead in leaps, going past what remained a cognitive, philosophical desert in Devorah's own mind. Perhaps she was simply too young and would take an interest later in thought like this.

They sat at the base of the crack in the rock, feeling coolness pushing out from its depths, comfortable with each other's silence for a good while.

22

IT WAS THE FEAST of Tabernacles, the feast that celebrated the time of wandering in the wilderness before the Jews had come into the land on which they now had a toe-hold. Aviel loved this time of year, because the entire household would build a booth of sticks outside and decorate it with dried flowers and berries and wild grasses. Meals were taken out here, under the stars, commemorating the forty years the people had wandered homeless and yet been provided for by Adonai.

Devorah had gone back to Capernaum, and Aviel missed her sorely, particularly because this time of year had always been fun for them when they were young. But they kept up writing, and Aviel promised she would come home for a visit at some point.

Yeshua and John and the rest had come back once briefly to Jerusalem, but it was so short that Aviel and John had not had the opportunity to see one another before Yeshua decided they should go back to Galilee for Pesach.

This time, however, Aviel had had word from John that they would be returning to Jerusalem for Sukkot and staying at his house; he expressed his desire to see Aviel in a delicate parchment letter sealed with dark blue wax, delivered by a small courier boy.

Yeshua has been speaking out constantly—so many people listen and follow, but there are so many others who are trying to arrest him. I don't know that your uncle would approve of us seeing one another, but I am so worried for Yeshua and what will happen—and you should come and see him speak, then you'll believe in all I've been writing to you about Yeshua. Meet me at my house, first light, two mornings from now and we will go hear him speak in the Temple.

Aviel stood in the atrium in the still heat of the day, folded the parchment, and placed it inside her inner garments just as Mordechai and Nicodemus came in.

"Still writing, my dear?" Nicodemus smiled at her, bemused.

"Yes, my lord. My uncle indulges me, and at the same time drives me to be letter-perfect," she responded.

Mordechai only shook his finger at her, and as the men faded into one of the back rooms Aviel heard Nicodemus exclaiming to Mordechai that Yeshua had told him he needed to be born again. "Who can understand this?" he put to Mordechai, as they faded out of earshot. Because sound did not carry well in the stone abode, Aviel could only eavesdrop so far.

Two mornings later, the temperature climbed fast and early as Aviel rinsed her face in the bowl, then wrapped her blue linen mantle about her. She almost wished she could go without clothes on days like this. Even the lightweight cloth clung to her legs already sweating in the heat of the day.

She was nervous; she had seen the outside of John's house, but had of course never been in, and had never lingered. While he wasn't wealthy, it was clear he had enough, and a few times she let her imagination run away with her as she fantasized making a home with him. As she walked, a stray barking dog interrupted her reverie, and soon she had climbed the small terraced hill to stand in front of John's wooden door. A single knock and he threw open the door, in awe of her back-lit beauty as she stood before him. Impulsively, he put his hand to the hair lining the side of her face and brushed it back under the mantle.

"Come. Let's go hear Yeshua speak. He's been doing this most mornings."

As they walked, their hands brushed, and it was all John could do to keep from grasping hers in his.

In a street up beyond them they suddenly heard some wailing, and since they were going the same direction, John picked up his pace and put his arm on Aviel's back as if to hurry her along as well.

A keening sound preceded them. Soon the cause came in sight: a woman with long curled dark hair but nothing else covering her was being dragged up the street towards the Temple by some scribes and Pharisees in their prayer shawls. Her banded feet scuffed the dust as she alternately stumbled and walked, trying to cover her exposed pubic area with her hands. Once, she turned her head and Aviel could see dirty tears streaming down her face, and Aviel recognized her as a young woman whose husband, according to the gossip, had completely turned away from her when she did not produce any children. Aviel supposed the woman had sought human solace, and so she had compassion for her, but then she looked at John, who shook his head, and only trotted faster to follow the company up to the Temple.

Despite her shock and embarrassment for the woman, Aviel winced as she saw one of the elders pinching the woman's arm, obviously hurting her in his disgust. An insect whirred past Aviel's head in the heat, and she could feel the woman's shame emanating beyond her in a gauzy haze. Finally, they reached the place where Aviel could hear Yeshua's resonant voice instructing the silent crowd, people listening raptly as dry leaves rustled on a faint breeze.

The elders began to part the sea of people in bright clothing, rich and poor alike who had gathered from their homes and abandoned their stalls in the Stoa to come congregate around Yeshua. Aviel could see the woman's head bend farther down onto her chest as she tried in vain to cover herself from the onlookers' eyes, which first dropped, then furtively returned to stare, sidelong, at the woman. A murmur had arisen, and Yeshua's voice was stilled.

Aviel saw Yeshua rise and turn to the woman, his gaze moving from the people to the elders. Silence. The elder who led her, and who even from the small distance smelled of garlic, pushed his thumb under the woman's arm and thrust her forward towards Yeshua.

"Teacher." His tone demanded. "This woman has been caught in the act of adultery. Now: in the Law, Moses commanded us to stone such. What do you say about her?" His malice was barely veiled.

Yeshua took a step toward the elder. Aviel felt the heat of the day, as if it would press the young woman and the crowd in toward the young rabbi. The crowd was colorful: embroidered swaths of cloths adorned the women, binding their waists, in contrast to blue woven pattern of the *tallisim* the elders wore. Aviel turned with a slight rise of jealously, expecting to see John staring at the woman's form, but instead he was focused intently on Yeshua.

The woman shifted her weight, swaying from one foot to the other; she looked as if she might drop to the dust, but instead her hands clasped her breasts to flatten them further into her chest. She must wish she could be out of her body, thought Aviel with empathy, this woman who was at the mercy of the clothed people. Aviel knew the consequence: would they take the young woman to be stoned, or burned, or strangled immediately?

With the ease of a young man Yeshua stooped, his robe sighing about him. Because she was a scribe, Aviel's attention was drawn to his hands: long fingers, graceful, like a scholar's, yet sturdy from his trade. His fingers wrote in the dirt. Then he straightened up and said, "Let him who is without sin among you be the first to throw a stone at her." Aviel knew his voice, but it had a new, thunderous, commanding effect on the audience. He had apparently come into his own more since she had last seen him.

Again, he bent down. He kept his head focused on the dirt; he did not look at the men who confronted him. Aviel saw a sign of life in the woman as she saw her eyes move cautiously around, though the rest of her body appeared as stone. People begin shifting, stepping up on tip-toe, peering over each others' shoulders to look at what the rabbi had written.

The elder's tight fingers peeled from the woman's arm, and he started another question—but then released it in a breath as he leaned forward slightly to see the writing in the dirt. Straightening, he glared at Yeshua, but then his eyes dropped, and he turned to leave. Yeshua continued to trace a finger in the dust, never glancing up.

Then, miraculously, the other elder at the woman's side turned to go. Next people began to drift away into the heat, one by one. Silence cloaked Aviel and John, and they withdrew along with the last of the crowd. John pulled on Aviel's arm and they ducked behind a stall with a cloth covering it. Aviel watched incredulously as John found a hole in the material through which to watch what Yeshua would do. Her curiosity no less than his, Aviel found her own weakness in the fabric as well and peered at the scene unfolding before them.

Yeshua stood to speak to the woman, and Aviel realized that the draw to which John had referred, and the pull from Yeshua that she had herself experienced in Capernaum, was far deeper than charisma could ever be. It was as if a calling-out emanated from his very bones, a calling-out that countered the woman's earlier keening. Surely this resonant cry echoed throughout all of Israel wherever he went, thought Aviel.

"Woman, where are they? Has no one condemned you?" His voice was quiet; his eyes bore down on hers.

The woman opened her mouth to speak, but nothing came out—only a breath of sadness. Then the woman raised her head and looked off to the side at the rabbi's shoulder, seeming to find the different, thicker-woven country cloth of his tallis greatly interesting.

Aviel and John realized they were looking at a woman who had, as the elder had accused, committed adultery.

"No one, Lord." The woman's words were barely audible. Then Aviel and John heard Yeshua's remarkable reply:

"Neither do I condemn you."

The young woman gasped a breath; Yeshua's voice compelled her to look up. Aviel knew and comprehended that connection through the eyes with Yeshua, because she had been subject to it herself. She knew that as the woman raised her eyes to look into his, she might die a death other than the one she had expected.

Still, the woman looked. And when she did, Aviel witnessed the adulteress's confusion as if she were watching her own, in retrospect, from the standpoint of an observer: she saw the link to Yeshua's power and depth, its disorienting and rare quality. And so the young scribe relived that moment at which all of her heart had been exposed to Yeshua.

The warmth of the day breathed for both women—in, out. Aviel could see the naked soul before her soften to a place with no words as she let him in through her eyes, and she saw peace clothe the woman. She was sure John also witnessed it. Then, Aviel had to look away, as if she were invading a private moment, or else see the woman immolated by Yeshua's clarity. John dropped his head, stunned.

"Go, and sin no more." Yeshua reached out to the woman and offered her his tallis.

Next Aviel felt John's hand tugging hers, but she was shocked to find how he had in essence disappeared from her awareness during the whole scene.

They crept out from under the stall and retreated down the hill, back towards his house, walking faster and then trotting, not speaking. The woman had departed in another direction covered with Yeshua's tallis.

Numb, John and Aviel stood outside John's house, facing each other in the private alley and out of breath from their retreat. The stone of the buildings around them had begun collecting the day's heat, radiating it outwards as they stood in front of one another. John recovered his sensibilities first, and began searching Aviel's face. She could only look down at the dust in the street, almost as if she had put on the skin and soul of the first guilty, then forgiven, woman she had just taken in. But when she did look up at John, she rested in his gaze, completely encompassed as in a pool.

Perhaps the sight of the naked woman had aroused the passion in both of them; perhaps the tension from the now-dispersed crowd had contributed to their feelings. Yeshua's surprising decision had left both of them off balance. John was confused, feeling a mixture of attraction to Aviel as well as to the extraordinary man he had been following for so many months. He was standing so close to her in the vacated and silent street that he could smell the lavender scent that was as soft as he now began imagining her skin to be. As his mind turned from Yeshua he raised a hand and sought out hers.

He began disrobing her in his imagination, laying her down on his bed, his hands playing over the curves he had first felt that day in Capernaum. Her hair cascaded over her shoulders, and he wanted to delve his hands into it to dishevel it and unravel it again. He swallowed and looked aside, not able to meet her eyes.

Aviel saw what was happening in his mind. She also knew that, all else aside, from a practical standpoint there was nothing to inhibit their actions right now. She was not able to become pregnant. She knew that John was aware of this. They were standing in a quiet side street, its other inhabitants absent. Other than what they had just seen, and the law and custom that informed them morally, there was nothing to turn them aside from going into the house together; no one knew where Aviel was right now; she was not expected anywhere. Neither moved.

Their tension did not dissolve as had the scattering crowd. It hung there, a tangled ball of passion held in the air in an upturned hand.

Then, drawing in her breath deeply, Aviel said, "Look at me." Their love had grown from an initial attraction and recognition of depth in one another, through contemplation of one another in the months and years apart, through mutual admiration in the letters they wrote. The lust of their youth had played no small part. Society, the society that would have broken the sinning woman had it not been for Yeshua's forgiveness, provided them life-giving boundaries. Aviel's discontent with Capernaum notwithstanding, neither of them chafed in any large degree at staying within the expectations of their social order. But what Aviel found in John's eyes defined the direction she at last knew she could, and could not, take. The love of his Lord pierced his eyes and soul more deeply than she could expect to penetrate him. He loved his Lord first.

He reached out for her, feeling her withdrawal. Though her heart would forever be fused to his, her face contorted in anguish as she pulled back from him and whispered, "Don't touch me."

She turned and left him standing there.

He stood, emptied, outside his door, legs weak. He squeezed his eyes shut, hearing her robes fade in the distance, and knew he had just made a choice for the remaining years of his life.

Back out in the main flow of people, Aviel turned in the direction of the Sheep's Gate, her eyes welling, her heart tightening in grief. She ran blindly, past the beggars and the lame, as she groped for the writing booklet at her chest. Once again, she wanted to die, at last.

23

Jerusalem, 36 C.E.

IT WAS A YEAR later. Mayreet, more silver-haired and generally achy all over, but still cheerful, had gone to the market to bring back some cardamon for later preserving the lamb that would be soon slaughtered. Aviel offered to take over mixing the spices when the older woman asked for help in the kitchen. A half hour later, with Aviel enjoying herself in more Passover preparations, Mayreet burst perspiring and agitated into the atrium and came running back to Aviel.

"They've taken Yeshua! There were people following him to Golgotha, where the Romans string up the criminals!"

"What are you talking about? Slow down!" Aviel gripped Mayreet's shoulder and plunked her down on a bench. Crucifixions had been on the increase, and Aviel knew that Yeshua had come into Jerusalem a few days before, crowds flowing about him like a stream, chanting and waving. He was not the only prophet going about promising the Kingdom of God as the Romans tightened their hold on the region, and none of those prophets had come to a good end.

Aviel and John had not exchanged any letters since he had left the year before, so she was unaware of the group's whereabouts or its agenda for their visit this time. She felt a tingle in both her hand and her spine at Mayreet's mention of the group of men and what was unfolding.

"Here. Give me the cardamon. Let's finish this up and go find out what's going on."

Mayreet looked blankly at Aviel but handed over the small packet. Her fingers fumbled and she spilled some of the mixture for the meat. They worked silently, a foreboding dangling on the air, then rinsed their hands and went to get their mantles. They slipped out without telling anyone where they were going.

As the women half-walked and half-ran down the narrow streets the clouds pressed down grey as if a rolling pin were flattening them out to cover Jerusalem. Mayreet recounted what she had heard about Yeshua's arrest, and how he had been questioned by the high priest and then the governor of Judea. Not only had the elders not stood in his defense, but they had acceded to Pilate's decision to crucify the young man.

Aviel stopped in her tracks at one point as Mayreet was telling the story, then shook her head and continued on. It stood to reason. No one who redefined power in the way Yeshua had, the way that Aviel had experienced firsthand, could be expected to survive long in a world whose foundation was, by all appearances, human will and control. Yet she had thought he might somehow overcome, somehow take his miracles and message to a broader audience, and live on for many years as a revered and wizened elder. She again shook her head as Mayreet chattered on their way out the gate to the area so commonly used for crucifixion.

At first when Aviel had come to the city she had turned away from knowledge of this torturous method of death for offenders of the Roman government, but as she had continued to live under the pressing regime it had become impossible to ignore.

Crucifixion struck her as bizarre: it was a crude, primitive means of effecting death, combined with cruelty, cheapness, and spectacular intimidation. Criminals were set on display as examples, that was clear, intended to stir fear in the populace and keep them in line. But death this way took a long time, so no one who had the normal human reaction of being drawn to gore really ever had the time to wait around to see the crucified die of asphyxiation. Yes, there was some blood after a person would be first tied to the cross, then sometimes have nails driven through the hands and feet, but the nails were gratuitous because it was really the tying that attached a person to the rudimentary crosses constructed of trees. The Romans would have done much better to hack off people's heads in public, Aviel thought, if they wanted to draw onlookers and frighten them into obedience. She had realized that the Romans were keenly aware that mercy and brevity were closely related. With crucifixion, simple hanging body weight drew down on a person until the lungs could not counter gravity to take in breath. It was simultaneously an unremarkable and cruel expiration.

Even the day was slow, as if the very air had gone thick with agony. As Mayreet and Aviel came upon the scene, they saw clusters of people gathered under the dark clouds, and tremendous scuffing of the dirt in the area as if a fight had broken out a while ago. Through the crowd, Aviel saw John and a group of women standing about twenty feet from the base of the cross on which hung Yeshua, elongated. Mayreet gasped. Aviel's eyes could settle on neither the pain on Yeshua's face nor the anguish on John's. Weakened at her knees, she clung to Mayreet's arm and moved closer to the group standing with John. Unending weeping penetrated a palpable faintness in the air.

First, Aviel averted her eyes from Yeshua and watched John as the darkness gathered. She could see the muscles in his throat working. Tears had dirtied his face and dried on it; he had not bothered to wipe his face. His eyes were blind as he watched the man he loved, the one who had brought life to so many, die before him. Aviel saw more lines around his eyes on his brow than she could have accounted for, given his youth. He must have become wearied by the last year with its struggles and losses.

As if he sensed her stare, John turned in Aviel's direction. Their eyes met. Recognition struggled with an unfathomable distance. In that gap Aviel turned to look at Yeshua.

As she forced her gaze to stay on him, she recognized herself in him: his face was flickering between the exquisite human fear of death and the release of that fear, which she knew from her own experience. At the end of a pulse, peace consuming his face, he turned to look for John, as if he would bring John up close to him and embrace him; then spasms of pain worked their way through his body again.

Yeshua spoke to John, drawing John's eyes, which had stayed on Aviel. Yeshua's voice had lost its thunder as Aviel heard him say something about John caring for the woman next to him, but Aviel could see the strands of attachment between John and Yeshua.

Omnipresent, Aviel's grief hung. Dying on the cross was suspended the man who had given her life, but also taken it from her in the form of John's human love. John had been charged now with the care of another woman, a mother, a woman Aviel had no knowledge of. Once his Lord was gone, John was to care for a woman who was already a mother.

Had he ever been meant to love a flesh-and-blood woman from the first time she had met him? She knew he had wanted to touch Yeshua through his heart and soul more than he had wanted to touch her, but he had wanted to touch her physically, too. Perhaps, because of his youth, or maybe because of his impetuosity, he hadn't known fully that the love of the One would crowd out the love of another, but he had discovered it, and at her expense. John had not known himself well enough. This was not an error for which he would repent; only with time and distance would she be able to forgive. But she would remember the remaining days of her life lived alone. Her bitterness before the dying Yeshua weighed against the love she felt for John, and her heart wrung with the contrast.

Drying blood, dimness, and the oppressive clouds filled the place, so Aviel took Mayreet's arm and drew her away, as Yeshua began taking the last labored breaths common to those dying on a cross.

As the two women made their way back towards home, Yeshua cried out. The sky turned a peculiar yellow, as with a dust and wind storm. A loud wind rent the walls of the side canyons as it rushed down into the surrounding area. As the women reached home they ducked inside.

Aviel slunk to her room, weeping.

24

Madison

ON A CRISP FALL day of leaves changing colors and dying, Jonathan drove out to the stables the Monday of the funeral for his niece, having brought a change of clothes. He stepped out of the car, rolled up his pant legs, and his shoulders fell. He almost began crying right there; he had brought the wrong shoes.

Slogging his way into the barn Jonathan found the stalls quiet and only partially occupied, so he made his way out to the corrugated metal enclosed ring behind the stable.

He pushed open the door to the ring gently. In the large open space four of the biggest horses ran rampant, wild horses on the hoof, as if at the mouth of a canyon. Manes were flying as they moved in perfect step-flight, circling. Jonathan leaned on a metal pen called the squeeze chute, watched, then let the pounding of the hooves shroud his sobs for several minutes.

Moira entered through another entrance, saw Jonathan's shoulders moving up and down, and brow furrowed, considered him. She waited a decent interval, then made a show of opening the oversized creaking wooden door. She moved a few steps toward the cohorts and turned her shoulder away in a subtle, least-resistance method of inviting them to her, extending an arm with some pellets in hand. She didn't look at Jonathan but knew he could see her.

"Look at you, you'd think you were a bunch of wild husses outside! We started offering our kids sweet treats to get them to do what we wanted, and they got obese. So maybe now we'll do the same with you, end up with a bunch of fat husses!"

The leader slowed, bringing the rest of the group up short. He approached cautiously, coming to lip the pellets out of her hand. She clipped the lead line to his halter and began peacefully leading him out of the ring, leaving Jonathan without having greeted him. A threesome of buddies informally named Huey, Dewey, and Louie followed, and a young woman who had come in after Moira clipped Huey as he got in range.

But number three, Dewey, properly named "Half Pint" on account of his size, stopped abruptly when he saw Jonathan. Moira and the other woman had gone out with the first two, leaving Jonathan alone with Half Pint. Half Pint was only about thirteen hands, with petite hooves, long eyelashes, and a long, wild mess of a mane, like a Spanish woman whose lover had tangled his hands in her sultry hair during his ardor. Half Pint was distinctive, but all together, the group had showed they were pack animals, flowing and following the leader seamlessly, fractals of the spirit of Horse. Half pint was stumped without his group, and was easily bribed when the young woman came back in a few minutes later.

Jonathan followed suit, wanting to be part of the horse group himself at this point. Back inside the stable, horses munched contentedly at their buckets in the corners of stalls as the aroma of hoof pickings and last night's piss wafted up from the floors. Seeking out Moira, Jonathan found her sifting manure from sawdust with a large-tine fork and dumping it into a battered wheelbarrow in one corner of a stall.

"Well hello there! Long time no see, Jonathan. Feel like shoveling a little manure? I need to get in a couple of the husses from outside. What are you doing here, anyway? Everything okay with Anna? I thought she was still away in Israel." Moira's voice was cheery, but face was pale and she had bags under her eyes this morning.

"She is. I guess I just sort of missed her and thought that this would remind me of her," he said lamely. "And I'll be happy to help. Just let me know if I'm doing it right."

"It's horse crap! There's not much you can do wrong," she chuckled as she went out to bring in Gold and Reno, his one-eyed buddy.

As Jonathan silently scooped the large mounds into a wheelbarrow, he wondered why horse turds were so much larger than a moose's. It didn't seem right. But then, many things didn't seem right at the moment. Since his niece Tina had died and Anna had been gone, Jonathan had lost sleep and had begun organizing all his pencils and rubber bands and paper clips in his desk drawer while accomplishing little else. He had no children; he could as die as easily his young niece, and while he didn't have as much of a life stretching before him as she'd had, he still felt he had much to accomplish and love to give. The one thing he had managed to get done was redrawing his will. Petting Maisley absently last night it had occurred to him that by coming out to see the horses he might get in touch with that vital part of Anna he loved so and find some comfort.

"This horse is the definition of fear," said Moira, as she brought Gold by the halter into the hall outside the stall in which Jonathan stood. She gestured to him to come out, and he swapped places with the horse. "He hasn't exactly gotten much worse since Anna's been gone, but he hasn't gotten any better, that's for sure. He misses her, I think," and looked at Jonathan.

Jonathan's eyes widened at her, and he didn't know what to say, then began explaining what had happened to his niece.

Moira listened. They mucked out stalls side-by-side, the barn close and quiet and warm. He tried telling Moira what he loved and missed about Anna so much. He kept pulling up strands from his subconscious, sketching an existential concern for Moira, but not giving her anything definite to latch on to.

Horses were smarter than people, she thought, and simpler, too. Smarter because they couldn't lie to you.

"I know about husses, and the only things I know about life, I know by extension through them. It may not be much, and the older I get the more I realize I don't know diddly squat. Now, I also don't know fully what your motivation is." She paused and leaned her bent frame on the cleaning pitchfork. "So you should take this for what it's worth, but it seems to me you have something to address with that young woman. Who's not getting any younger." Moira's wrinkled eyes came over a broken section of stall wall and looked squarely at Jonathan one last time.

Stalled in his babbling, he just looked at her, then Gold, and Half Pint. He took in a deep breath, then smiled at her. He thanked her for her advice, as she did for his labor, then he exited the barn and changed outside the car for the funeral.

He finally knew what he needed to do.

25

Israel

"EDNA? THIS IS ANNA, from Madison—I met you on the plane coming over to Israel. "

"Hi, hon! How you doin'?"

"Just fine, Edna, just fine. Actually, I saw you at Yad Vashem too, but I didn't want to disturb you."

There was silence on the other end of the phone, then a sigh.

"Well! Dear. What can do for you?"

Anna launched into her story. Edna stayed awake throughout the entire story, ooh-ing and ah-ing at the climbing descriptions, quiet at the mention of Nir, and overall entranced by the description of Anna's find.

"Would you be able to come and have a look at it for me? You'd need to come to the outdoor education school at Ein Gedi, not Jerusalem—I'll be going back there. Tomorrow." Anna added, "I mean, I don't know if that's the right thing to do, and it may be nothing, but I'm just so curious . . ."

"Well, you might want to call whoever the antiquities authorities would be—I don't know much about that—but I was planning on coming to the area anyway, and now you've got me curious, too. If you'll just hang on to the item, I'd certainly be delighted to look at it, dear. I think there's a bus going tomorrow. You know I can't drive, of course."

"I'd be happy to pay for a cab for you if it doesn't work out; just let me know."

"Okay, dear, but I'm pretty sure the buses will run there. It takes a while, a circuitous route, you know, but I'm pretty sure I can get there. I'm wanting to make a visit to the Dead Sea again. Been floating in it yet? It's truly strange! You float higher than in any other water. Just let me find out what time I can get there, and I'll give you a call back, okay?"

They finished, and Anna went to her room to begin packing her things. She carefully wrapped the item in amongst her clothes, then went into the kitchen to rummage for some fruit and a piece of chocolate-and-vanilla-marbled halvah, the faintly sweet, compacted paste made from crushed sesame seeds with honey as a binder. She came back to her room and ran her finger slowly over the clay container.

Nir had come to pick up Anna in the van the next morning, and they had had a lively ride back to the school, talking shop and mightily ignoring the sensations that had passed between them the other day. For her part, Anna felt as if she had a secret and did not tell Nir about her find. She did have to somehow let him know about Edna, though.

"By the way, I met this woman on the plane. She's a funny sort, but I wanted to get together with her again, and she told me she's coming to soak in the Dead Sea. Any chance the school can put her up, maybe in my room? I don't mind sharing."

Nir's face fell, then he recovered.

"Sure, no problem, or if she wants a room to herself we can charge her a lot less than a hotel would. And she can pay al la carte for any food she wants from the cafeteria."

"Thanks." Anna looked sidelong at Nir, wondering how it was she had so managed to crowd Jonathan out of her mind since she'd been there.

Edna arrived, wiping salt sweat from the continually evaporating Dead Sea from her brow. She gave Anna an expansive, voluminous hug and made mixed sounds of admiration and puzzlement at the school designed to work young bodies so athletically. The mere thought of it exhausted her. As soon as she had plunked down her suitcase in Anna's room she was anticlimactically asleep on the lower bunk bed. Anna began moving her own things up to the top bunk.

Once Edna was awake and refreshed with some fruit and sparkling water that Anna had sought out for her, Anna fingered gently through folded-up clothing to find the clay vessel. Edna may have been compromised somewhat physically, but this belied her intellectual and educational prowess. She pulled out reading glasses, and together the two women delicately took off the top of the clay canister and pulled out the tiny papyrus scroll.

"At first I couldn't figure out what language it would be, but the more I looked at it, the more I began to figure it was Hebrew. Is it?" Anna questioned her guest.

"You've had this out already? And touched it and put it back in? Do you realize how fragile this is? The only reason it's not crumbling to dust under your fingers is that, well, now we're more in the desert . . . it must have been so dry where it was kept in Jerusalem . . . but it's wet there, and these things just don't make it over time. Was there sand in this? That may have made for a dry enough environment for it."

Edna's thought process was a little hard for Anna to follow, but the young woman was keeping her patience and piecing together what she thought Edna meant.

Edna gasped. "Oh my, glory be! Will you look at this!" As they unrolled the ancient paper Edna's eyes grew large. "This is a letter. It's from a woman."

"Can you read it to me?"

"Okay: Aviel, daughter of Jairus, to Polycarp . . . Daughter of Jairus? How can this be? Do you have any idea who . . ."

"No, and who's Polycarp? Is that some kind of fish?"

"Oh for crying out loud, no, girl. Polycarp was a bookbinder and seller, from early Christian days. The most recent theory is that he knew John the apostle when John was very old and Polycarp was very young. They hit it off. Because Jesus' kingdom of God hadn't been ushered in during the lifetimes of the disciples, John, among the writers of the other gospels, figured he needed to write down what he had witnessed about Jesus. Now, you gonna let me finish reading this?"

"Okay, okay, it's just I have no idea about this stuff. How come you know so much about this early Christian era? And know Hebrew, for that matter? You didn't indicate on the plane that you were such a scholar."

"I don't look like one, do I? Well, turns out this is very important to me. Not just what I learned in church from when I was coming up, but what I could learn on my own. And the more I learned, the more I wanted to learn. There's the language, the history, the archeology . . . but you know, the more I learn, the more I realize I don't know. Still, it's all very interesting. I learned Greek, and I even started learning Aramaic, in between snoozes . . ."

"Is that the old language Jesus spoke?"

"Yes, although most Jews of Jesus's time were learned in Hebrew, being the literate people they were, and of course they conducted a lot of their business in Greek. And you know, it was the wealthy women in the cities who were often the most learned. They had the time and the means, you know."

"No. I did not know that."

"Well, in any case, let's get back to what this woman has to say!"

They resumed:

Aviel to John. Greetings in our Lord Jesus Christ.

This finds you after long years—if it indeed makes it to you; I give it to my sister to deliver safely to you. I have news frequently of you, of course, given your ministry in Ephesus. I have been having more and more trouble writing, and I cannot see well I cannot see . . .

Here the script ran at a right angle off the page, then picked up again on a new line.

I have not been well, and my memory escapes me. Sometimes I am told I make no sense when I speak. Old age has been rich, but such a withering in these final days I did not anticipate. It seems I cannot die even yet, but my mind dies a slow death

I leave no children behind, as you know. I have served the Lord through my scribal work in these latter years, but I do not wish for my words to live on beyond me, as we talked about. Please, honor my wishes in this. Please dispose of this letter in a manner you can de you yyy

Anna and Edna looked at each other, Edna shaking her head. They made out what they could of the next section.

But I ask the Lord for my mind to steady as I continue:

I understand you intend to publish a book with Polycarp that you have written about the Lord. "I would enjoin you to respect a few of my concerns. You know that I have loved only one man, you, John. I beg you in the spirit of this love, whatever your memory of our time together is—even now I can feel your palm on the side of my face.

You gave me your word long ago that if you ever decided to commit to written word any of the details of Yeshua's story that you would alter details to protect my identity. Whatever anyone else might write, I know your heart well enough, even though it was so long ago, I know it well enough to know you to be a good man such that you would use your influence to ensure that the story will either not appear or I will certainly not be named. This grace of anonymity I ask of you; it is within your power to grant it. It is our Lord's name that should be known. Forgive me; I cannot repeat myself enough.

"But this letter never reached John," said Anna.

"Shh." Edna would not be interrupted.

Now, next, in what you write. You may indeed use the shortened versions of words for the sacred names of our Lord and Christ, the abbrevi-

ated scribal forms to which I introduced you. At first, after the Lord had touched my hand, I thought I had begun using the shortened forms because we eliminate the vowels from the name of the Holy One when we write, and also because the Greeks shorten many words.

Yet we use these because they differentiate our movement from the old scripture. At the same time, because they are distinctive, they will cause each scribe hereafter who uses them to contemplate God in new ways. These contractions bring together the most important parts of the Name. Each letter is like a person, joined above with our Lord overarching. There is a beauty in simply contemplating each one. Without the Lord above, two letters, or two people, will never come together.

You and I were unable to do this.

Anna's eyes narrowed at the words, and she recalled Jonathan's mild denunciation in the living room in Madison.

Then there was another gap in the script, as if Aviel's memories filled a space on the page. Then the letter continued:

The focus, when a reader reads these names, is to be on the Name—not on the author of the name, not on the individual letters of the name.

Each written name is a prayer, a focusing. Each time the name is written a grace comes over the scribe. I know. This is how I came to know the Lord as Lord instead of simply Yeshua, whom we all knew in life. This grace is the only way I am able to continue writing now, as I forget from one moment to the next what I was writing. I commend you and others of our following to this practice. These names are sacred.

My hair is gray, my skin dry, John. Perhaps you would recognize me by my eyes. I have spent my life in the company of myself, and in my yearnings to die and be released from the daily pain of losing myself and all those whom I love. I only ever had two flowing springs in my life—the well of my love for God, which poured forth from my hand, and the love I kept pooled in my heart for you. That dried like the parchment on which I have written, and will blow away with the dust of my bones. I am old. I ache. I ache to die. And yet even now I cannot reach it as I once thought I could, because I know now that I will be resurrected in the Lord.

If you are committed to seeing your writing through, and it will make the world a better place, then follow it with the passion you would have shown in loving me. I am not so sure it is such a terrible thing to put aside love of another human being if you have passion for a vision.

Anna bit her lip and looked out the window up into wadi.

I would have been a better woman if I had been able to accept the grace of the Lord sooner. Would you have been a better man had you been able to love both your Lord and me?

I suppose what I have wished for all my life is not so much death as it is peace. My body, I expected, but I didn't not think my memory would get so like this.

I have asked my sister, Devorah, to take this to safe keeping if I do not recover to se

Edna looked at Anna, then out the window; both were speechless.

"Do you know what she's talking about? Who was she? What . . ." Anna couldn't get all her questions out at once and reached for a wadded up Kleenex in her pocket.

Putting her hands to her cheeks, Edna began explaining. "This is the *nomina sacra*! She's the one who invented the *nomina sacra*. Oh, my God. This is historic. Do you know what this is worth? This is easily worth a few million dollars. I wonder if you'll be able to sell to a museum? The State may just claim it. We have to tell someone. You could be rich, Anna."

"What do you mean, the *nomina sacra*? Slow down! We're not telling anyone. She says right here she doesn't want her words shared." Anna hopped from one foot to the other, like a child having to go to the bathroom.

"This is important stuff, young lady. Look. Old manuscripts, before the printing press. Scribes did them all. Most scribes were men, but some women were trained because they had beautiful handwriting. What you have to realize is that most people of ancient times were not literate. So anytime they wanted to convey something in writing, whether it was a bill of sale or a love letter, they had to hire someone. It was a job, a profession, back then.

"The Jews were the most literate society because they taught their children—of course, male children mostly—to learn Hebrew from a young age since they had to learn the Torah, the Hebrew Scriptures. By the way, it's really very condescending of Christians to call it the Old Testament, but we do. And in Jesus's day, they also learned Greek because it was the language of commerce. If you wanted to do business in Jesus's day, you had to know Greek. Then, of course, they spoke Aramaic, sort of an odd form of Hebrew, not too unlike Yiddish in idea, and so a really well-versed scribe would know at least three languages.

"Both the Greeks and the Jews used contractions for certain words—

the Greeks for mostly anything, and the Jews for the sacred names of God. But I'm getting ahead of myself. Give me a second—I'll get back to that.

"So it looks like we have a lady scribe here, name of Aviel. She says she's Jairus's daughter. Anna, you could give her her name in history. Ever notice the women in the Bible who don't have their names? Lot's wife, the Samaritan woman . . ."

Here Anna interrupted. "Is that the girl I read about in the story you had the Bible turned to when we were on the plane?"

"Yes. You remember it?"

"Sure."

"Well, she wouldn't have been permitted to be a Torah scribe because according to tradition only men did that, but she would have been able to be employed by Jews, Romans, Greeks, practically anybody. But what's more phenomenal is that she knew the apostle John, and very well, it sounds like.

"And," Edna continued on, almost out of breath and nowhere near falling asleep at this point, "there's a new theory out there that this Polycarp was the actual publisher of the first edition of the New Testament, and that he knew John."

"What do you mean? Weren't there four different authors of the New Testament gospels and the Church chose to put them together at some point, leaving out other ones, like the Gnostic Gospels and the Gospel of Thomas?" Anna could barely keep up with Edna's quick and dirty history lesson on the formation of the New Testament. She was also more interested in the personal life of the woman whose words they were reading.

"No. All wrong. The four gospels in the New Testament are attributed to respected people at the time. But the truth of the matter is that no one knows precisely, with certainty, who each author or authors was or were. We know Paul wrote some of the earliest Christian correspondences, but after that, apart from a whole lot of words from scholars who have almost as hard a time as doctors saying 'I don't know,' the best we can do is make highly educated guesses as to when the gospels actually came out and who penned them. You have to be careful. Scholars are a squirrely bunch; they know just enough to be dangerous.

"One thing, one fascinating thing, however, that we know from scholarship, is something that distinguishes early Christian texts from all others of the time. Remember, there was a lot of literature going around those days, and there were booksellers just like we have today—just not in the same volume, of course. No Border's. The amazing thing is these *nomina sacra*."

"Well, I remember enough Latin to know that means 'sacred names,'" said Anna.

"Right! Well, they are contractions, like I was talking about a minute ago. Like 'don't,' 'wouldn't,' 'can't.' You get the picture. Except that what they're contractions of is a lot more important! Mostly they're collapsed names for 'God,' 'Lord,' 'Jesus,' and 'Christ.' Later on they contracted more words, like 'savior,' 'son,' 'spirit,' 'heaven,' and so forth and so on. What they do is distinguish any document of the time as uniquely Christian. So what it would look like in English would be, say, if you wrote 'G' and then 'd' for 'God' and drew a long line over the top of 'Gd.'" Here Edna drew her example, then continued, "Just as kind of an aside—I don't want to bore you with this stuff."

"No! No, this is fascinating," protested Anna.

"Well, okay. Christians also used the codex, a book form, instead of the scroll. Before that the codex was mostly used for informal writing, not fancy literature. So, anyway, if you were looking at old documents, and came upon some of these codex pages balled up and stuffed inside a book cover to pad it out, which the old scribes used to do with the pages they made mistakes on, and you saw these contractions, these *nomina sacra*, you'd know you had a distinctively Christian document right off the bat. That actually happened, by the way. This guy who came and lectured at our church once found some pages that way in a library one time. Made the papers, it was that big a deal. So what you're looking at here is something that attests to the person who actually created the idea of contracting the names! And it looks as if it might be one of the characters named—or, that is, not named—in the scriptures. A woman."

"That's preposterous," objected Anna. "First of all, how likely is it that something this old survived? And then second, how likely is it that I found it?"

Edna laughed and placed both her hands on her knees. "Well, maybe you've heard the story of the shepherd Bedouin boy who discovered the ancient Dead Sea scrolls in the jars inside some caves not too far from here, as a matter of fact. He threw a pebble one day into this hole in the rotten rock walls that are pitted with openings. The pebble hit something that sounded funny, so he scrambled up towards the cave (he was supposed to be looking for a lost sheep) and he made arguably the greatest discovery of the twentieth century. A splinter group of Jews around the time of Jesus had hidden old manuscripts in jars inside these caves near their compound when the Romans threatened them with extinction. The scrolls could survive because of the extreme dry conditions—like the mummies in Egypt.

"Well, after the manuscripts were discovered, caves nearby got raided by other Bedouin and lots of scrolls ended up on the private market before things settled down and fortunately the majority of them—we think—found their way to museums. But talk about unlikely. He throws a stone into a hole? You couldn't write a movie like that and get away with it. Unless you had Nicolas Cage or Harrison Ford starring in it."

Anna snorted and turned to look out the open doors up into the wadi. She wondered about the curious, and yet probably in most ways very ordinary life, of the woman who had written the letter. What was she doing on the day she, or her sister, had placed this letter in its clay container in the crack at Gai ben Hinom? Certainly she hadn't had technical climbing gear. Anna could only imagine her appearance, her cares and losses and joys. That she had loved was clear. John the apostle, no less. And that she had believed fiercely in someone, and something communicated itself in her missive too. Yet out of all this improbability, the unlikelihood that the two of them should be connected down through time, Anna heard most clearly the request of this woman to remain quietly anonymous. She wondered why it had been so important to her.

Anna turned around and looked at Edna, who had finally fallen asleep. She carefully lifted the scroll and put it back into its container, then tucked it into her camisole under her shirt. It felt cool against her skin.

Next, she heard a knock on the door.

26

ANNA OPENED THE DOOR to see Jonathan standing before her. Grunting, Edna woke.

Anna's startled reaction initially overrode her pleasure. Jonathan faltered greeting, but Anna recovered herself quickly.

"Jonathan! What on earth are you doing here! Hi! Hi." Anna guarded the letter's container by turning her body slightly as she moved to hug him.

Their embrace was peculiar but familiar as well. Behind Jonathan stood Nir, who watched the exchange. Anna saw him looking down in embarrassment. She tried to introduce them, but it was clear they had already met and Nir had in fact ushered Jonathan to the room.

"Hi Anna," Jonathan said lamely.

"Come on in! Nir, come on in too. Have you met Edna yet?"

Edna turned from watching the expressions and body language of both Jonathan and Anna, grinned broadly at Nir, and extended her hand.

"Pleasure, I'm sure."

"Welcome to Ein Gedi. Any friend of Anna's—" and here Nir turned a pained expression to Jonathan.

Edna had a curious smile playing about her face and was wondering what exactly were the relationship complications here that were creating the uncomfortable space wafting between all the parties. Except for her.

"I'm going to just step out for a breath of the desert salt air, if you will excuse me," she said formally, and she and her hips swayed down the corridor.

"Uh, Anna, I've opened another room for Jonathan down the hall, and let him know he can make himself comfortable. He can just pay cash at the cafeteria." Nir's voice was flat.

"Thanks so much—this is quite a surprise, Nir. Did you know Jonathan was coming?"

"Anna, I didn't know I was coming. I needed to see you," and as Jonathan said this, his vision seemed to focus so solely on her that Nir faded from the background. Nir felt the shift and simply turned quietly out of the room, following Edna's retreat.

"We just talked . . . is everything okay? What's going on?"

"I had to come, Anna. For me. I mean, for us, just . . . Look . . ."

Anna interrupted him. "Sit! Get comfortable. For heaven's sake. Can I get you anything?"

"No, listen, it's all been so confusing since the funeral. I've been thinking about the funeral nonstop. Some of my thoughts have been really dark," here he glanced at his feet under the bunk bed, "and it just seemed like it would be better to talk with you in person instead of just racking up the phone bill. It's not the same." He pleaded with her in a way she had not seen from him.

Anna sat next to him and put a hand on his back, then brushed the hair from his forehead as if she were comforting a child.

"Thoughts about death? About how it could happen to us?"

"Yeah. And just all the grief. It's like it's sticky, it sticks to you. And it's heavy. I can't get out from under it. And it would be the same for us, if it happened. I mean, with the house and the stuff and even Maisley. No one in either one of our families would take care of our things the way we would for each other, but we're not married. So you would lose big time if I died. Because we're not husband and wife. I just can't quit thinking about it. I want us to get married, Anna."

"Because we might die suddenly?" She moved away from him slightly and her spine straightened.

"Well, yeah, but not just because of that. You know why. I thought it wouldn't sound right on the phone, so I figured I should come here to tell you. You can travel as far away as you want, but I can't get away from wanting you."

Standing, Anna went and looked up the wadi. The air was so still that she thought she might actually witness God passing by at that moment. Her heart and breathing were steady, peaceful.

Jonathan's solidity, which she had always likened to the rock, had become an impossibility. Had his belief been ever-growing, their relationship would have worked for her, but he was the resistant one now, more so than she. It was resistance of a different sort than hers, more internal, almost a defiance of his own growth of belief. He had come smack up against his fear of death, and something in his handling of it, his impulsivity in coming to Israel and the quick solution he sought, frightened her.

Her resistance was more an external shell of habit born long ago, one that covered an ever-shifting internal landscape. His was more entrenched. With her trip to Israel and now the death, they had become like two magnets that could not be forced together, repelling each other's opposite field of attraction.

As she stood in the silence she realized that the ability to work change in oneself, like the change she sought in her kids and her horses, was more life-giving than the rock-solid safety she had sought in Jonathan. In the final sum, what had appeared solid in them as a couple really wasn't: it was brittle, like the manuscript she held close to her body. Edna's depth of spiritual conviction, the commitment of the Israelis living in this land, and the burning intensity of the letter from this woman Aviel, moved Anna beyond words far greater than love-making with Jonathan ever had. Dimly, then painfully, she acknowledged to herself that this was backwards. She turned back to him and contemplated him.

On the one hand, she didn't want to write off this man she'd known for so long and who had known her as well, more thoroughly than any other human being. It would hurt; it was sad. It was plain to her now that Nir was just a last-minute diversion from what she had grown to know she needed to go more places than Jonathan could follow. Her traveling had simply been her body's pursuit of the truth she deeply knew. Taking a deep breath, Anna did something that neither one of them had ever achieved fully with one another, despite their having shared living space, details of their lives, linens, body fluid, a happy dog. She spoke from her heart.

"Jonathan, if your belief in us were great enough you would have moved on it long ago. I think we both know we haven't really been going anywhere. Together."

At first he didn't know how to react. Then his thoughts came out in a rush not so much because he couldn't stand her actual words but because the sincerity of what emanated from her soul burned his denial so cleanly, leaving no ashes.

"Does this have anything to do with that Nir guy? Have you gotten . . . involved . . . with him?"

"No! for God's sake. Don't be stupid. You know me better than that. Yeah, sure, the guy's good looking, but it doesn't have anything to do with

Nir. It has to do with the power of belief I've seen since I've been here. There's passion here. It's all around me, I'm suffused with it. Even the rock I climbed sort of releases it, as if it absorbed it for thousands of years before anyone touched it.

"That passion, that conviction is as old as the layers of the land," she continued. "It finds its expression too often in violence, in addition to celebration, but the people here, they're alive. They're not stone." She watched her tongue so as to not hurt him. "They're like the kids and the horses I work with. They may be a little intense, but they're okay with it, and operating fine. The people here may also be off track some, about what they focus on, but they are focusing so fiercely on what they believe that it's—it's life-giving.

"I need that. We don't have it. Can you tell me honestly you think we've had that?"

Again her words burned his heart. His denial wrestled his nice-guy image, and neither was coming out the clear winner. Shoved up from his depths came a realization that part of him had gone for the drama, this getting on a plane for effect. But his heart and head were so out of touch with one another that he couldn't accept the information, so he plunged it back down deep inside of himself. He floundered.

"What do you want me to do? I came here . . ."

"You came here out of a supreme lack of clarity. You're looking for a savior. You're not aware of it, but you expect me to play the part even though you don't know you're asking me to take it upon myself. What kind of a catch-22 is that for me? Can you even begin to see how shackling that is? It'll take both of us down if we try to build something permanent on it. It's not only not enough, it's not even healthy." Her words had grown more heated.

The one way Jonathan did know how to respond—though it was out of fear, not righteousness of heart—was with anger. He shouted at her, "You stand there and tell me to my face that we haven't had passion? That I'm not clear on why I got on a plane? You're just pulling the same old crap again! You've avoided me all this time, not letting me get closer, not being willing to marry me. You're the one who made the catch-22, not me. Then you dangle this other guy in my face . . ."

For a few moments Anna froze in the bathing ferocity of Jonathan's you-accusations, reminded of her mother's rage when she was a child, but then gradually, eerily, she floated up above it. He'd come an awfully long way under the pretense of love just to fling blame at her. On his next reloading inhale she left the room quietly and with dignity, looking straight down the hall and moving towards the outside light. As she exited the building she heard Jonathan bleat out a cry for her. But he did not come after her.

As Anna came outside, she saw Edna sitting in the shade of a palm tree, appearing to listen to the silence as if from it she could discern some wisdom. When Anna stopped before her, Edna spoke with deliberation and kindness.

"This is a land steeped in loss, hon. It's hard not to feel it in every nook and cranny. It's almost a mood or a way of being that anybody who lives here has to accept in order to exist, I think. It's a sociological phenomenon. Since everybody else here suffers and loses, you might as well too, right?" She shook her head and looked Anna directly in the eye. "But I think you need to consider carefully before you do anything you might regret later."

Anna swallowed and looked hard at this woman she hadn't known very long. "I need to feel I have integrity, Edna! I need to act with as much integrity as Aviel did. If I can't seal my own choices against time and scrutiny, including my own losses, in this holiest of lands, where can I do it?"

"I can't answer that for you, hon. But I believe you have the answer inside of you." Edna smiled up at her. "Who knows? Maybe you can show some of the rest of us the way," she said.

Anna merely looked at her and then tears began to roll down her face. She turned, and breaking into a trot she ran straight across sand and rocks towards the Dead Sea. Her tears dried on her face as she ran, and emotion came in waves over her as she realized what she was losing. Her own fears rose to the surface, coming as swiftly as a review at the end of life. As she got closer to the salt-encrusted rocks she had to slow her pace, but her heart was still beating rapidly and her breath came in heaves.

Even with an overcharged system she had a mental reserve of cool lucidity that had come with her decision. A few times she lost her footing and put out her hands to catch herself on the salt crystals, bloodying herself. She cried afresh, knowing she had to throw away so much in order to get what she knew was the only choice that would work.

At the edge of the water, Anna stood and steadied herself, gaining her footing. She picked up a small stone. Putting all her force behind it, she threw it out as far from shore as she could. You throw like a girl, she thought. Tough.

She perched uncomfortably on a rock and breathed in the smell of the brine all around her, as if the Dead Sea contained all the tears of all the Israelites over time. Pulling the clay vessel out from inside her shirt she turned it and tapped the parchment out one more time, getting some blood on its edges. She opened it slightly and looked at its contents.

Clearly, if this piece of paper was really what Edna said it was, it was valuable beyond measure. Probably she could get in a lot of trouble for messing with an antiquity. She thought of the letters of Mother Theresa that had recently been discovered and published for all to read, even though Mother Theresa had expressly requested that what she had written be destroyed. Mother Theresa had also been known by name, unlike this woman—or unlike the Samaritan woman, or Lot's wife, for that matter. Anna sensed something significant in the woman's anonymity.

She didn't know if Christianity, or history, would be better or worse off without those letters from Mother Theresa, and she hadn't read any of what was actually published. But she did know from looking at this letter before her that the woman clearly would have considered it a violation for this letter to be released to the public. Wouldn't it be greater truth to adhere to the wishes this woman pleaded for? When she had put the letter into the crack in the rock, or when her sister had, she had never believed for a moment that it would be found and exposed to scrutiny.

Anna wanted her own desires to be held just as private. She understood what Aviel meant about two people needing God overarching them, and she and Jonathan didn't have that. It wasn't that their faiths were different—that would be a challenging yet possible scenario for a couple she supposed—it was that he didn't seem to want spiritual growth in the equation at all.

She gave up a sigh to the setting sun. As if putting her signature on the internal shift, she put the letter back in its vessel but left off the top. Aviel would remain Jairus's anonymous daughter, as the scripture read. She stood, then flung the clay piece hard out into the sea.

The container sailed out farther than she had ever thrown anything and landed with a soft plop on the buoyant salt sea. For a moment it sat. Then slowly, inexorably, the water swallowed the parchment.

www.ingramcontent.com/pod-product-compliance
Lightning Source LLC
Chambersburg PA
CBHW050404030726
47503CB00006B/2022